To my family: Writing this book was the most healing experience ever! I'm so blessed by all of you and your support.

1

Chapter One

The mystic that the burned and tattered country church held for Jenny was more than any curious six-year-old child could resist. She was constantly sneaking off across the field of hay at her Grandparents farm to investigate the structure. Every time she would be caught by her Grandmother, every time she was reminded that 'to spare the rod was to spoil the child'. Gran was half Cherokee Indiana and all Scottish temper. She could be a kind woman at times but being the mischievous child that she was, Jenny seldom saw the softer side of Gran. More often than not Jenny ended up on the receiving end of her godly discipline. Despite her 4'8" small frame, the switch that Gran used could bear mighty welts to the back of Jenny's legs. No sooner would the sting wear off and the welts fade, Jenny would be on her way back to the old church once again.

One particularly cool fall morning, sweatshirt in hand, Jenny managed to slip from Gran's watchful eyes. This was usually pretty difficult to do, Gran could see like a hawk. Today, Jenny had an advantage. Gran was too busy with chores and five other grandkids under her feet even younger than Jenny. Gran knew Jenny could take care of herself as she had witnessed Jenny's independence on several occasions. Being an only child Jenny was use to fending for herself and Gran knew it so her focus was more on the younger children. Sneaking out the side door, careful to not let the screen slam shut, off Jenny ran across the field.

The church smelled particularly musty that morning, probably the dampness lingering in the air from the rain storms the day before. The leaves from the big oak tree next to the church had fallen into the pews from the burned out hole in the roof, making it seem as if the *outside had come in* to Jenny. It seemed to be even more comfortable and peaceful to her this day. Jenny felt at peace with her surroundings, she loved this old church with the deep grains of wood on the pulpit still visible though the top of it was covered with soot and damp ash. There just seemed to be a 'presence' here that made her feel comforted and loved. She felt safe here. Exploring the ruins of this old burned out church was her favorite pastime.

Grandpa Jake had told her he would come with her when he had the time, hoping to keep her from slipping off on her own and getting hurt. He didn't want to quench her curiosity, but the old structure had been severely damaged by fire a few years back. Why no one had bothered to tear it down was a mystery. Maybe because it was a 'country church' and it wasn't the eyesore in the country that it would have been in town.

How great it felt to Jenny to be off on her own! She truly disliked being around the other cousins at this age. Not that she didn't love them, but the older ones were bossy and would have told on her if they had seen her sneak away and the younger ones she would have to 'watch' and help 'babysit' if she were found. She didn't want to babysit her cousins. She just wanted to explore 'her church'. There wasn't a pew she hadn't imagined people sitting in. There wasn't a song she hadn't tried to sing at the top of her lungs from behind the old pulpit, thankful that no one could hear her but Jesus. She was alone with him here, and that made her feel warm and fuzzy all over.

Today she found an old Bible that had been damaged by the fire and weather. It was torn and moldy from age. She couldn't read it. Heck, she was too young to read much of anything. But she knew it was Jesus's book and she just couldn't leave it here in the damp burned out church. It just wouldn't be right. So she clung tightly to it and lying down in a dry pew, she fell asleep. Sound asleep, that is until she heard footsteps!

"Oh NO!" She thought, "Gran must have found me! I'm going to get switched all the way back to the house!"

She tried to sneak out of the broken window in a side room. Ever so quietly she lifted her leg up and straddled the window sill. Then she nearly wet her britches when someone grabbed onto her leg! She let out a scream that could have scared the devil himself away.

"Shhh, Jenny-girl, be quiet! If your Gran catches us here she will switch us both!" It was Grandpa Jake.

Relieved it was Grandpa, Jenny swung her other leg back into the church and flung her arms around her Grandpa's neck. She was indeed his 'Jenny-girl' and to her, Grandpa Jake was her best friend in the world, and her protector. He protected her from Gran and her evil switch on more than one occasion. When she needed a place to run to that was safe, Grandpa Jakes lap was a sure bet.

"Grandpa! What are you doing over here?" Jenny asked as she smiled and batted her big brown eyes at him. She knew her eyes were her secret weapon with Grandpa. He told her she could talk her loudest with her eyes.

"Saving the likes of you from your Grandma is what I'm doing here! Gran is hunting you with a vengeance with a long willow switch in her hand. Figured the only way to keep your backside from being switched was to come and find you myself." His blue eyes of steel were looking out the window in search of Gran. "I know your Gran is mad enough at you right now to switch you all the way back to the house and back again, she may even decide to switch us both if she has a mind." He chuckled.

The image of short little Gran switching big, tall Grandpa made Jenny giggle.

Grandpa Jake saw the Bible Jenny had tucked up under her sweatshirt peeking out.

"What have you there Jenny-girl?"

"I found this today Grandpa, isn't it just so beautiful?"

Taking the tattered, moldy Bible from Jenny's hands, her Grandpa turned the pages gently. Jenny could see a tear in the corner of his eye as he now faced the pulpit staring up at the lopsided cross hanging above it.

"What's wrong Grandpa?"

"Nothing child, it's just been a long time since I held the good book in my hands." A kind of sadness came over him that Jenny had never seen before.

"Grandpa Jake, please don't cry." Jenny reached for his hand. "Jesus loves you, that is what it says in that song I heard them sing at Sunday school. Did you ever come to this church Grandpa? Before it got burned?"

"Nah child, I never was much for going to church, too many chores to be done. Sunday is just another work day for me."

"But, don't you believe in Jesus Grandpa?"

"Jenny-girl, the good Lord doesn't just live in these buildings. He is everywhere. I talk to him when I'm working in the woods, I talk to him working the garden, I see him everywhere."

"You SEE JESUS?" Her eyes got as big as two chocolate drops from the five and dime.

"Sure baby girl, just look all around you. You can see him in the flowers, in the new baby animals. You can even hear his voice on the wind if you just listen. You don't have to go to church and sit on these old hard seats to know that there is a God Jenny."

"But, shouldn't people GO to church grandpa?"

Not wanting to dampen the girls obvious longing for the Lord her Grandfather said; "Yes child, if they can, they surly should."

Then Grandpa took her hand and pulled her onto his lap.

"Jenny, if I never teach you another thing in this life, I want you to remember what I'm going to say to you now. Listen closely to me girl."

Jenny had never seen Grandpa this serious about anything before. He was generally a quiet man, working hard and talking little. He would sit quietly in his chair on the front porch after a long hard day at work, whittling out a new toy for one of the grandkids with his pocket knife. This was a very different side to him she was seeing, she listened hard to what he was going to say.

"When I was a youngster, my Ma taught me this verse in the Bible. Not a day has gone by I my life when it hasn't given me strength."

"Is that why you are so strong Grandpa? Cause you're STRONG Grandpa!"

"Not a physical strength Jenny." He put his hand to her heart and tapped her chest. "I'm talking about spiritual strength. Strength, that is in your heart."

"I know you can't read much of this good book yet. But I want to show you a verse, and I want you to remember it Jenny. It is Romans 8:28, in the New Testament. When you get older, you will see that life isn't always so easy. Things can get hard, that's just how life is Jenny. There may even be times if you wonder if Jesus is even real." Grandpa was leafing through the old Bible as if looking for the page.

"No Sir! I won't! I know Jesus is real!"

"Trust me Jenny. There may be a time when you may wonder about that. Just listen to me and trust me."

"What does it say Grandpa, the part your Mama showed you?" Jenny asked.

"It says this." Grandpa turned to a page and pointed. Jenny learned later in life that Grandpa Jake had memorized it, because he could neither read, nor write.

"All things work together for the good, to those that love the Lord." Sighing he asked; "Do you know what that means Jenny?"

"No Grandpa I don't."

"It means that no matter what happens to you, a good thing or a bad thing, that something good will come from it in the end if you love Jesus." He hugged his granddaughter close. "Remember that Jenny, if you love Jesus, even the bad things that happen to you are for a reason and God will make something good from them."

Peace fell over Jenny as she listened to her Grandpa Jake talk. She didn't understand very well what he was talking about, but she knew she would remember the verse. And she knew someday she would read it for herself. God had his hand in her life even at the age of six. And on that very day when Grandpa Jake told her about the book of Romans, Jenny decided she would live her life for Jesus. She hugged Grandpa Jake's neck and gave him a big kiss on the cheek. Then out of the blue, the peace of the morning was shattered by Gran coming into the church, switch in hand!

"I'm gonna blister your little bottom Jenny Nicole White!" Gran shouted as she swung the switch into the air, making a swishing sound as it sliced through the silence. It made the hair on the back of Jenny's neck stand up!

Gran was marching toward her and in her fury she grabbed Jenny by the arm so hard it jerked her clean off her feet! Rearing her arm back to strike, Gran was ready to follow through on her threats of a good blistering!

Just as Gran was about to come down across the back of Jenny's legs, Grandpa Jake grabbed her wrist. With a stone cold look in his steel blue-gray eyes he said; "If you lay one hand on that child woman, it will be the last thing you ever do! Never again, do you hear me? Never again will you hit this girl." He shouted.

It looked to Jenny like a stand-off of two angry bulls! But Grandpa Jake was the bigger one and he wasn't to be reckoned with when he was really mad. He had made his point very clear and Jenny could not remember another switching from Gran from that day forward.

Years later Jenny named her second son after Grandpa Jake. Pride was in his eyes when he was handed his great grandson to hold. "Little Jake" Grandpa called him.   Grandpa Jake passed on when little Jake was just two-years old.   While Jenny never saw her Grandpa in church, other than the burned out one. She knew he was a man of God. The way he lived his life reflected Jesus. The day   he   died,   she   lost   her   best   friend. Jenny never forgot that beautiful fall morning when she was just six-years old. She never forgot the scripture she had told her about. Although she read it over and over again as she was growing up, she never dreamed it would literally become her lifeline to God.

Chapter Two

Jenny curled up comfortably under her favorite quilt as she sipped a cup of herbal tea. She gazed mindlessly out of the window.

Will this ever be over? She wondered. She had been living in a nightmare for over five years now and she simply wanted it to all end. She wanted to move on with her life and put it all behind her.

But Jenny knew there was something she had to face up to first. She had to face what had happened to her, all of it. And she had to stop blaming God.

Since she was a small child she had always kept a journal. It was a good thing she had. The only way she could recall all of the events in the past five year the way they really happened was to refer to her journals.

Jenny had been working at a medical center in a southern Michigan college district. It wasn't a huge trauma center, just your average 'middle town USA" medical facility. Thirteen years ago she had made surgery her career choice and was now a Certified Surgical Technologist. She loved her job and was very proud of her profession. A career in surgery isn't for the weak in spirit, or the weak stomach!

When she had first made her decision to return to school, her husband, Rob, was more than a little concerned. Rob wasn't sure she would be able to juggle raising two sons, schoolwork, keep up her end of the chores around the farm and take care of the house all at the same time. But Jenny did manage, just fine.

Since she was a little girl she had wanted to be nurse, the thought of working anywhere but the operating room never once occurred to her. Whenever company came to her house they were immediately treated to an examination by 'Nurse Jenny.' She would check their heart with her toy 'stefacope' and take their temperature. They always left with a bandage whether they needed it or not.

All of her stuffed animals were destined to a scar where she had opened them up just to see if their stuffing was ok.

One spring day her small collie became sick. It was just the usual puppy upset stomach. But Jenny was sure she needed surgery. Taking her pup to a secluded corner of the front porch, she proceeded to cut her hair. Thank goodness her mother heard her as she impatiently scolded the pup for not holding still!   The dull butter knife and round tip scissors did nothing more than give the pup a bad haircut. Jenny however, got a spanking although she insisted she had just saved the poor pups life!

There had been seventy applications for admission into the School of Surgical Technologists when she applied. She was sure she didn't stand a chance of being one of the five accepted. After all she was now a twenty-seven year old mother of two growing sons. Her interview had gone well considering she was not only late for it but covered in mud when she arrived. Just as she was pulling out of her driveway she happened to catch a glimpse of Rob trying to round up the horses. They had broken through the gate and were now roaming free in the field that had no fence to keep them from the road. She couldn't in good conscience or good sense drive off and leave Rob to catch tem himself. Naturally, it had rained all night long and the field was a muddy mess, so was Jenny when she got back to her car. If she had gone in to even change clothes she would never make the interview.

Pamela Easton didn't hold that against her. Once Jenny explained to her what had happened, Pamela simply laughed it off. She felt that Jenny must really be determined to become a surgical technician to come on to the interview despite her muddy clothes.

Weeks went by and each day Jenny would check the mailbox for news of her acceptance. She had put forth many prayers asking God to help her be accepted into the program. When the envelope came, she was nearly too nervous to open it! She did and she was accepted! Joy flowed through her as she jumped up and down in the kitchen of their small farm house. Finally, she was going to have the career she had dreamed of since childhood!

Classes were difficult at first. There was anatomy, physiology; psychology and microbiology, there were all kinds of 'ologies'! Not to mention surgical procedures, sterile technique, instruments, hundreds and hundreds more instruments! Her mind was becoming mushy and she began to doubt her decision to go back to school. When she would doubt, she would remember that God never gave us anything that was too hard, too difficult to handle. He never put on us, more than we were capable of.

On one of the more difficult Friday afternoons, the instructor announced that the next Monday morning they would actually be going into the operating room to watch a surgery! That weekend Jenny could barely sleep, her adrenalin was rushing as she anticipated Monday morning.

Before they left on Friday, their instructor, Pamela, had given them something to think about.

"Some of you may discover that you simply aren't cut out to work in the operating room, you may find you don't have the stomach for it." She had said. She warned them about temperamental surgeons, flying instruments, yelling and swearing such as they may not have heard before. It all made Jenny stop and think. She had never really seen anyone hurt badly before. She wasn't sure if the sight of blood would affect her or not.

Monday morning as Jenny lay awake watching the minutes drop off the digital clock on the nightstand.

Everyone was excited as they walked down the hall to the surgical suite. Pamela Easton, their instructor, was a fiery red headed Irish woman whom the students affectionately called; Ma Easton. She was full of energy and jumped constantly from one subject to the next so fast you could get whiplash trying to follow her. At least once a day you would hear her use her two favorite expressions; "According to Hoyle" and "When the shit hit the fan!" Shit hitting the fan sounded like an interesting concept and Jenny wondered if she would know it when it happened.

Not about to let them go into the operating room on an empty stomach Ma Easton led her students to the nurse's lounge and handed them a list of the scheduled surgeries for the day. She was letting them pick which surgery they would observe on their first day in.

"WOW! We are in the nurse's lounge!" An overly excited Josie exclaimed.

"Well, touch you!" Beverly said as she playfully touched Josie's arm.

"This is so neat!" Jenny giggled. "Do you think anyone will know we are students?"

"Oh of course not," Lisa teased. "Unless the read the word 'STUDENT' that is tattooed on our foreheads!"

"Yeah, there's that, or unless we walk around all day with our hands straight up in the air in fear of touching something sterile." Denise chimed in.

"Since I am the 'eldest' and the mother of two grown men, I declare first choice by reason of seniority!" Beverly said. "I want to watch an open-heart surgery. We don't see them in our little hospital and I want to take advantage of being able to observe one."

Beverly was indeed the eldest. She was also a Licensed Practical Nurse, currently working in the operating room of a small hospital nearby. The administrator there had submitted her name to the class, wanting her to have the more specialized training that could be offered to her at Community General. Bev was a good student despite her claim to temporary memory lapses she often termed her 'brain farts'. Bev had a wonderful since of humor and often led the rest of the girls into mischief.

Josie was an ex-cop with two small sons and three ex-husbands. She was a good person, just a lousy judge of men. She and Jenny had gone to high school together and oddly enough, here they were in the same surgical technology class, all these years later.

The girls all laughed with Josie when she announced she wanted to watch a hysterectomy, simply because she wanted one! Only Josie would use that kind of logic to determine the first case she watched in the operating room.

Denise was the baby of the group, fresh out of college with a Bachelor's Degree in Chemistry. Even she found the one-year surgical tech training grueling. Denise liked facial surgery and chose to watch the repair of a fractured mandible that had been shattered in a car accident.

Lisa was the genius in the class. Earlier in life she had been an Army LPN, a Certified Hypnotist, an Acupuncture Therapist and a Spiritualist. Not to mention a self-declared 'white witch'. She was the funniest person Jenny had ever met. Lisa said you had to have a sense of humor to raise two kids and be married to the same man for twenty years!

Jenny and Lisa had hit it off immediately. It was odd to both of them that they felt such a connection. They seemed to be able to read each other's mind, even when they didn't want to! Although Lisa's new-age theology and her spiritual beliefs concerned Jenny, their friendship grew. Lisa was raised in the Lord and Jenny was determined to remind her that Jesus was the only way to salvation. Finally, to preserve their friendship they agreed to disagree on religion. They became known as the 'Chip and Dale' of the O.R. Where one was, the other was close by and always with a smile or a joke to tell.

As Jenny sat on her sofa reminiscing, still sipping her tea when she closed her eyes she could almost see them as they sat in the nurse's lounge that day. The 'Five Amigo's' were about to embark upon the halls of the surgical suite for the very first time. They laughed at how they looked like Smurfs in their blue scrubs, blue shoe covers and blue hats and a blue mask over their face. All that could be seen of them was their eyes. Yes, they indeed looked like the Smurfs.

"Jenny," Lisa bubbled with excitement. "What are you going to watch as your first surgery?"

"I haven't decided yet." Jenny replied. "But I want to see something REALLY bloody." Her concern over seeing blood for the first time was growing and she might as well nip it in the bud, so to speak.

"Let me see that schedule again." Lisa glanced over the list of cases as if she were placing an order for Christmas. "Ahha! Here, an above the knee amputation. That should be bloody enough for you!"

"Do you think Ma Easton will let us watch it?" Jenny asked.

"I hope so. I think I can handle it, I probably saw worse as an Army nurse. What about you Jenny? Can YOU handle it?"

"Good question, guess there's only one way to find out and there is no time like the present." Jenny answered.

"Well, none of us are going anywhere on an empty stomach." Josie said. "Remember we were to eat first, and personally, I think that is a great idea because I am starving!"

Moments later, Pamela Easton came through the door to collect her students.

"Have you girls decided what you want to observe today?"

"Open heart." Beverly replied.

"Hysterectomy." Josie said.

"Fractured mandible." Denise chimed in.

"Above the knee amputation." Lisa and Jenny said in unison.

"Whoa, I don't know about that one." Pamela replied. "The only reason I am going to let Beverly watch the open heart surgery is because of her previous surgical experience. An amputation may be a bit too much on your first day."

"PPPLLEEAASE…." The two begged.

"At least just let us try, a little peek? I really need to know if I can do this." Jenny said.

"Although it is against my better judgment, okay. But only IF you promise to leave the room if you start to feel lightheaded or faint."

"Promise!" They agreed.

Pamela took all her students one at a time and placed them in their assigned rooms. Introducing them to the surgeons and nursing personnel as her students. When it came time to take Lisa and Jenny into their room she tried one last time to convince them that an amputation may be too much on their first day. Of course they didn't see it that way.

Pamela opened the big swinging door into operating room #3, her two students following behind. The room seemed *very large, and very blue*. The walls were light blue ceramic tile, the floors a speckled black and white tile. Bright lights were everywhere. It seemed that *whatever was not blue was silver*. All around the perimeter of the ceiling were very bright fluorescent lights and in the center of the ceiling hung large, even brighter spotlights. With the use of sterile light handle grips the surgeons could direct these brilliant lights directly into the surgical field. The operating table was directly underneath the spotlights in the center of the room. Surrounding the head of the table was the anesthesia equipment. The anesthesiologist manned the controls of the equipment much like a pilot in the cockpit of a 747.

The term 'circulating nurse' was used to define the non-sterile person that responds to the needs of the surgical team. They could be either a Registered Nurse (RN) or a Certified Surgical Technologist (CST). Their job was to record sponge and needle counts, document every aspect of the case in the patient's chart, and supply sterile supplies to the surgical team within the sterile field. They also interviewed the patient before they were taken into the room to insure we were doing the right surgery on the right patient! It was also necessary for them to shave the hair off the incision site if necessary and wash the skin with iodine solution. The circulating nurse was responsible for everything that went on in the operating suite she was assigned to.

The term 'scrub nurse' could also be either an RN or CST. The scrub nurse is the sterile member of the surgical team. Their responsibility is to prepare and maintain sterility of the instrumentation and the sterile equipment. Once the surgery began it was her job to hand the instruments to the surgeon as quickly and efficiently as possible. Any type of assistance the scrub nurse can offer during the course of the procedure was expected of her. She would be asked to hold retractors to assist with exposure, cut suture when needed, suction the blood to keep the field of vision as clear as possible for the surgeon.

First Assistants were most often the surgeon's own private nurses. However sometimes they were residents or medical students. Occasionally the surgeons would operate with the help of only the scrub nurse, as was the case today.

"You will have a great view of everything from here girls, just remember: LEAVE if you feel sick!" Pamela introduced them both to the surgeon and staff before she placed them at the end of the operating table, just out of the sterile field. "If you need me or decide you would rather see another case just have someone find me for you." She left without them even noticing she had gone.

They had a great view of every move Dr. Kyle was making! As he took the knife into his hand to make the skin incision, Jenny wanted to look the other way, but she didn't. She had to force herself to watch, she had to know if she could handle this. A line of blood trickled down the patient's skin. Jenny kept her eyes on it. She didn't feel sick at all, she felt fine. In fact, she felt better than fine! Anxious to see what was next, she shifted on her stool to get a better view. Dr. Kyle then began to dissect the tissue back, cutting through a thin layer of fascia, the layer of tissue that is directly beneath the skin, then through the fat. Once he was through the muscle he pushed back the layer of periosteum covering the bone, exposing it to prepare for the use of the bone saw. He was ready to cut bone now. The bleeding had been controlled by the use of electro cautery and silk ties, but as Dr. Kyle began to use the power saw, blood and bone dust mixed with sterile saline solution sprayed everywhere.

Neither Jenny nor Lisa felt at all queasy. Instead they felt exhilarated, curious and eager to stand across from Dr. Kyle himself and assist him.

Dr. Kyle was very nice as he explained every move he was making to them, but Jenny was having a difficult time focusing on his words. Instead, she was more impressed with the scrub nurse doing her job. Jenny watched her intently. Every move she made was so precise! The scrub nurse handed Dr. Kyle the instruments he needed *even before he asked for them! She anticipated his every move!* In that moment, in operating room #3, Jenny knew without a doubt she had made the right career choice. She wanted to be just like this scrub nurse. A skilled Surgical Technologist, a professional. After months of on the job training, doing every type of case, Jenny was finally scrubbing on her own without her wingman. Oh, her wingman was watching in the room now, but not scrubbed in right beside her as she had been over the past several months. It felt amazing! Months had passed, her skills were sharpened and it was finally graduation day!

Chapter Three

Butterflies swarmed in Jenny's stomach as she prepared for graduation night. She was a nervous wreck! She had never graduated before! Having quit high school when she was just sixteen to give birth to Robbie, her first son, her diploma had been earned through taking a GED test at the college several years later. This truly was her first graduation ceremony and she had been chosen, rather unwillingly drafted so to speak, to give the graduation speech.

The fact that any of them had graduated was a miracle in itself. Pamela Easton had been promoted to Director of Surgery halfway through their training. The girls were quite challenged by their new instructor and her technique for teaching them. One day mid-way through the program, all five of them joined together and marched into her office and quit school in unison! Of course they worked out their differences as it wouldn't do the reputation of the school well, to have all the students quit at once.

Considering all they had faced the girls got through it because of their sense of humor. It was really what got them through. They learned the names of the instruments by using ridiculous word associations, humorous poems and jokes were all their memory tools! It only seemed logical that their class motto became; "Illigiti non carborundum". Latin for "don't let the buzzards get you down." It was just as logical that their graduation speech was based totally on humor.

As Jenny stepped onto the platform to deliver the speech that she and Lisa had written together, she felt her knees weaken. Family and friends would appreciate the humor it contained as they understood that laughter was their way of getting through the classes. But would the rest of the audience understand? The hospital CEO's, the doctors and the other nurses that were there, would they understand? She hoped so; they above all should understand that you didn't survive life in the real world of surgery without a sense of humor. So, she began to read:

"We are the class of '81. At last an O.R. tech!

We managed to complete the year, our lives a total wreck!

They all said that we were different, as students we were odd.

And if we ever made it, we would owe our thanks to God!

29

We have done it all, we goofed real big, the list is never ending.

But if you bear with us awhile, we'll start at the beginning.

They stood in awe the day we became Dr. Anderson's advisors.

They lined the halls to watch us draw our first paychecks, the misers!

We hit the Code Blue button by mistake. They all came on the run.

We told them it was an accident, but they still went for the gun!

They laughed at our silly goofs, they will never let us forget.

We put the trash bag on the Mayo-stand, they talk about that yet!

Some controversy arose concerning our possible future.

How were we to know you had to LET GO of the suture!?

Doctor Sims was covered in blood, so we made him undress in room #3.

Then of course, there was the fire hose that no one but us could see.

We learned to survive cafeteria food and how to become really small.

The later was out of necessity. Our lockers were in the hall!

Poor Ma Easton held up well considering what we put her through.

But when the 'shit hit the fan, according to Hoyle', we knew what we had to do.

It hasn't been easy for us, or for you but now that our training is done.

We will wash the word 'student' from off our foreheads, and shout to the world we have won!"

After Jenny had read the speech she took the time to get serious. Thanking their families and friends, whom without their support the task of learning and developing their education would have been impossible.

Graduation night ceremony behind them they all went to the local restaurant with their families to celebrate.

No longer the 'student' it was now time to enter the real world of surgery.

Chapter Four

Everyone took a few weeks off before starting their jobs in the Surgical Unit, everyone that is, but Jenny. She showed up first thing Monday morning after graduation. It wasn't that she didn't need a vacation after all the time in school. She just chose to take one later in the month to be with Rob and the boys.

As she changed out of her street clothes and into scrubs that morning she wondered what it would be like without the support of the other girls. She was no longer going to have the privileges that went along with being a student. There would be no security blanket, no port in the storm to rush to. She was on her own. She could only hope that being the 'new kid on the block' that she would have an easy assignment. Maybe with one of the surgeons she had grown more familiar with during her training.

As she approached the desk of the charge nurse to pick up her assignment she could hear Dr. Lawton throwing a fit about something.

Dr. Lawton was an abrupt man, affectionately named the 'dancing bear' because he growled, cursed and paced the floor when he was upset. He certainly wasn't one of Jenny's favorites, he somehow always managed to make her feel inadequate.

Silently she prayed; "Please Lord, don't let me be in his room, not today, not my first day on my own." But as she reached the range of hearing what he was saying, she had no doubt that she was indeed in the 'dancing bear's' room.

"I don't need a new scrub nurse in that room! I want someone with some experience!" He yelled at Barbara, the nurse supervisor. "This patient is a personal friend of mine! He is a pillar of the community for Pete's sake! What the #%-+*%@$ do you think you are doing giving me a fresh graduate on this case?" His language reflected his sour mood!

"I'm sorry Dr. Lawton. I have no one else to give you. We had an open-heart scheduled this morning not to mention two total hip surgeries. All of the girls that normally scrub with you are tied up in other cases. Besides, Jenny was an excellent student, she will be fine." Barbara replied calmly.

"I want to speak to the director of surgery. NOW!"

Barbara dialed the phone and handed it to him.

"Easton, Lawton here, this is complete bull S###t!" He yelled into the phone at Pamela. "Giving me a news scrub nurse on a case of this magnitude, are you crazy!? If anything goes wrong I will have your job!"

Pamela listened patiently while Dr. Lawton screamed into the phone.

"With all due respect, Dr. Lawton, my job is my own. Not yours to have. Jenny will do just fine if you keep off her back. Now, unless you want to hire your own help for all of your cases I suggest you take who I assign to you without pitching a fit each time you don't get your favorite or usual people." She calmly replied to him.

Slamming the receiver down on the phone, he turned quickly nearly running Jenny over in the process. He walked away grumbling under his breath about having 'new scrubs' in his room.

Pretending not to have overheard the whole scenario, Jenny approached Barbara. "Hi Barb, what's with Dr. Lawton?"

"YOU are with Dr. Lawton. You are doing his case this morning." She could see the look of uncertainty on Jenny's face. "Don't let him get to you Jen, you are quite

35

capable of doing this case or I wouldn't have assigned you to it."

Panic was trying to settle in her body as Jenny scrubbed her arms in preparation for the surgery. Keep your mind on scrubbing your arms, she told herself. Thirty strokes to the fingertips, twenty to the hands, ten to the arms, concentrate on scrubbing. You can see the anatomy of the lungs so clearly when the patent is positioned on their side and the ribs are retracted back. Removing a lung was a challenging and very interesting procedure. Unfortunately the reason for removing a lung was usually cancer. When Jenny assisted Dr. Colter, she found them to be one of her favorite procedures. Just because Dr. Lawton had a far different personality than Dr. Colter, it didn't change the way the procedure was done. And the fact that this was a personal friend of the surgeon and a 'pillar of the community' meant nothing to Jenny. She did her best for every patient, no exceptions.

She silently said the name of every instrument as she placed them in the proper arrangement on her sterile back table. She then counted her sponges and suture needles with her circulating nurse. Checking and double checking the count.

"Relax Jen, this is a breeze!" Marilyn whispered as she helped her pull her sterile table to the surgical field.

Jenny thanked God that Marilyn was her circulating nurse. Marilyn was one of the most experienced professionals in the unit. Not only was she a darn good nurse, she was nice as well. Knowing that Marilyn had confidence in her ability made Jenny feel more confident too.

"Stay calm Jen, you've done this procedure many times, you know your instruments." Marilyn told her. "And remember, he is just a man! You aren't here to impress the good doctor. You are here for the patient's sake." Marilyn winked at her. "For the patient's sake Jenny."

Dr. Lawton made no attempt to hide the fact that he did not like having Jenny in his room. The feeling was mutual as Jenny wasn't thrilled about being there either! But she had a job to do, and by gosh, she was going to do it!

Sponge, knife, scissors, criles, cautery… she was anticipating his needs as if she had been doing it for years. The procedure seemed to be going along quite well. Then, just as Ma Easton had warned her it would someday do; "The SHIT HIT THE FAN!" There was definitely no mistaking it!

The disposable stapling devises that later were developed were now still reusable metal monsters that needed reloaded after each time the surgeon used them. They were not all in one piece as their new and improved versions. They were several pieces that fit together like a jig-saw puzzle.

She had her "TA55", metal monster of a stapler all loaded and ready to function. Dr. Lawton was going to need it to staple across the lower lobe of the patient's lung to remove the diseased tissue. Jenny handed him the instrument with great care, then immediately turned her attention to suctioning the blood to give Dr. Lawton a clear field of vision. However, when Dr. Lawton began to position the instrument for use, as he maneuvered it, it literally fell apart in his hands! As expected, 'when the shit hit the fan', Jenny saw a first- hand demonstration as to why Dr. Lawton was called the 'dancing bear'!

"Damn instruments never have worked right! The #*$%$#'s fall apart when you need them!" He shouted as he fumbled with hands that shook in anger, trying to put the stapler together again. "Put this G...D....thing back together for me!" He yelled as he practically threw the instrument in Jenny's direction.

"Did you even have the ^%&&^% thing together right in the first place?" He snapped.

He continued to dance around the room, stomping his feet and cursing at Jenny as she worked diligently to put the metal monster back together. Each time she would come close to getting it finished, the dancing bear would stick his fingers on it trying to grab it from her before it was secure, causing it to dissemble again.

"Well for God's sake Jenny! Can't you do anything right? He bellowed at her. Where had she heard those words before? Oh yes, Rob's favorite words to her. She began to fume! "HURRY UP! Do you even know what you are doing? Damn stupid people in this room!" He grabbed it once again before she was finished. Once again, it fell apart.

That did it! Dr. Lawton was no longer the only one angry in the room! Men, why do they think they can talk down to us this way? Who in the heck does he think he is!? I take this kind of verbal abuse from Rob, but she doesn't have to take it from a stranger and she will not!   She yanked the instrument back out of Dr. Lawton's hand with force and turned around to her back table where he couldn't reach it. With precision, she put it together.

"What the $%@% do you think you are doing?" He growled at her in a threatening tone.

"I'm putting this instrument together." Jenny tried to keep her tone calm.   "I DO know how to do it, my problem has been, I can't keep it out of YOUR hands long enough to do so!" There, she got it, handing the instrument back to him. "Your instrument is read, DR. LAWTON."

Marilyn smiled at Jenny with her eyes, giving her *two thumbs up.*

The case went well from that point on, for Jenny and for the patient.

As Marilyn taped the patients dressing in place and prepared him for transport to the recovery room, Dr. Lawton walked over to Jenny.

"Hell of a job kid, thanks for your help." He said.

Jenny was stunned. She was even more surprised when Barbara came into the room a few minutes later.

"What went on in here?" She asked.

"What do you mean?" Marilyn responded.

"Lawton just apologized to me for yelling at me about assigning a news scrub nurse to his room. Then he picked up the phone and called Pamela and told her that she had graduated one of the 'best damn student's' he had seen in years. He said that Jenny could scrub for him anytime!" Barbara smiled.

Jenny felt great! She had survived her initiation under fire into the operating room. She thanked God, because without Him, she couldn't have remained calm. She even felt the problems that had started to develop between she and Rob had helped her to stay calm.

Truth was she and Rob hadn't gotten along in a few years. He felt trapped by their marriage and he took it out on Jenny and the boys, verbally. He was never physically abusive to Robbie or Jake, just verbally.

Jenny knew she should leave, but she still loved Rob. And she was committed to her marriage for life.

After that first day with Dr. Lawton, Jenny was assigned bigger cases. Once the charge nurse saw that she could handle herself she was the one who got the difficult cases and the difficult doctors. But she didn't mind. She knew she could handle them. It gave her confidence. She loved the challenge that came with each new day in the O.R. Every day was a new day and every day was a chance for God to teach her patience, increase her strength and bless her with the chance to help others. Being a surgical technologist was everything Jenny had dreamed it would be. She loved her job.

Chapter Five

The phone rang at 2 a.m. Jenny was glad she slept in her clothes with her tennis shoes beside the bed. She was on back up call tonight. Normally on back up call you seldom were needed unless it was something 'not' so good. She grabbed her keys and ran out the door. The farm was a good thirty minutes from the hospital but past experience had shown her she could make it in less than twenty minutes. Her heart raced as she wondered what she would find when she arrived. When the call from the hospital operator had come in, she was too sleepy to as what the case was. She only heard the word "STAT" loud and clear.

Would it be a car accident, gunshot wound, maybe a stabbing? Perhaps it was an aneurysm, the possibilities were endless.

As she approached a curve on the highway Jenny saw the all too familiar lights of a state trooper in her rearview mirror. She pulled over.

"May I see your license please?" The trooper asked.

"I'm sorry officer, but I really don't have time for this right now." Jenny said as the officer gave her a 'look' of 'oh yes, you do!' "I'm a scrub nurse at Community

General and they need me in the operating room for an emergency case." Jenny explained to him. "Would you mind escorting me? Then you can give me a ticket when we get there if you still want to." Jenny handed the trooper her license and her Operating Room photo identification. "Seriously, this could be life or death."

He checked both of her identifications, and saw the sticker in the corner of her rear window that said: Surgical Technologist. He then agreed to escort her to the hospital.

Jenny could barely keep up with him as he ushered her through the red lights and city traffic. He pulled into the Emergency Room entrance at the hospital. He rushed from his car and quickly opened her car door when she came to a stop.

"You go on up." He said. "I'll park your car for you and bring your keys to the operating room."

"Thank you!" Jenny yelled back to him as she ran through the doors of the hospital.

"Just do a good job!" He waved.

Changing her clothes in record time, she stood beside Dr. Colter at the scrub sink. Just eighteen minutes after she got the call from the hospital operator.

"What's on the agenda tonight?" She asked him as they scrubbed their arms in unison. The patient was already on the table, already under anesthesia. Jenny could see Lisa quickly fluttering around the room as she prepared for the surgery. Lisa had been on 'first' call tonight. They often tried to back each other up as a team whenever possible.

"Let me guess, Lisa has the cardiovascular cabinet and instruments in the room, aneurysm?"

Dr. Colter shook his head. "Ruptured, as soon as we get into the room I want YOU to start preparing the graft for clotting. I'll give you fresh blood to use as soon as I can."

"How much has he lost?" Jenny asked.

"It isn't good. Not good at all."

As they entered the room Lisa quickly handed each of them a towel to dry with. No words were needed. Both Lisa and Jenny had become very good at their jobs and knew what had to be done. No need to waste time with words.

Jenny immediately began to help Dr. Colter drape the patient with sterile linens. Lisa began tossing off the suction tubing and electro cautery cord to the circulating nurse to be hooked up. They would be needed first. Jenny heard the snap of the knife blade going onto the handle just as Dr. Colter asked for it.

He was right. There was plenty of blood in this man's abdomen. Jenny suctioned as Lisa sponged as they worked in unison doing all they could to save the man's life.

Even with all that was going on around them, Jenny knew that something was bothering Lisa, besides the obvious. But there was no time for chitchat now, the patient was their priority.

Dr. Seever, the anesthesiologist on the case, was in his own world at the head of the table. He was doing all he could to stabilize the patient's blood pressure as he pumped in more units of blood to replace lost ones. He seemed to be fighting a losing battle.

"I'm afraid we are losing him Tom." He said to Dr. Colter. "He has lost too much blood. It is going out faster than I can pump it in."

They continued to work as fast as they could. Only seconds later Dr. Colter was able to clamp off the aorta. The patient's pressure stabilized.

"Is that graft ready yet Jenny?"

"Yes sir." Jenny had been clotting the graft with the blood Dr. Colter had given her moments earlier.

"Give it to me, we have to get this sewn into place and unclamp his aorta before we lose him."

Jenny followed his suture keeping it from tangling as he sewed in the graft. At the same time she was suctioning blood to keep the field of vision clear for him. The graft went in smoothly but they were still losing ground. He was still losing blood somewhere.

"I can't get a good pressure on him Tom." Dr. Seever said. "We're going to lose him."

Both Dr. Colter and Dr. Seever had done everything humanly possible to save him. Two hours had passed since the surgery began. The battle had been lost. There was no blood pressure, no pulse. There had been no response to the cardiac paddles. The patient was pronounced dead at 5:20 a.m.

Dr. Colter left the room after asking Jenny and Lisa to close the abdomen and clean the patient up. The family would then be allowed to view the patient if they chose to in a quiet area by the recovery room. Dr. Colter was going to go speak to them now; Jenny didn't envy the doctors that job.

As they stapled the patient's skin closed Jenny became increasingly aware of Lisa's mood.

"Lisa, are you ok? You haven't been yourself tonight."

As they pulled the sterile sheets back off the deceased man's body and began to wash the blood off him, Lisa whispered;

"I knew him." She pulled the IV out of his arm and tears began to cloud her eyes.

"Oh my gosh!" Jenny exclaimed. "How? Is he family?"

"No, he has been a friend of our family for many years. Jim and I use to play cards with him and his wife when our kids were little."

"Go home Lisa, I can take this from here."

"No, I want to finish this Jenny, I need to. You understand don't you?" Lisa asked.

Jenny did understand. She knew better than to argue with Lisa when she was determined to do something. She felt such pain for her friend. She wondered if Lisa was thinking about God now. She wanted to ask her, but this wasn't the time to preach to her friend. Losing a patient was hard enough, losing a friend like this was harder.

Death, you never get used to it. That was one thing about her job Jenny didn't like. The lives they couldn't save. She always wondered if the one's they lost were 'saved' through Jesus. Or was this cold brutal death in the operating room truly the end.

Chapter Six

The winter had been a long one this year. New surgeons joined the staff, new procedures being performed. That meant more new equipment to learn to use, the schedule had been so busy that the weekends were hard to distinguish from the weekdays. With one big difference, on weekends the operating room was staffed for emergencies only. That meant only one circulating nurse and one scrub nurse on Sundays. The term 'emergency' was being used rather loosely in those days with the caseload being as full as it was through the week.

Libby James was the circulating nurse on duty with Jenny on the twelve-hour weekend shift. They worked closely together and relaxed together when they could. Today was super bowl Sunday of 1991. Libby was a big football fan and Jenny didn't mind it. The two of them scurried around the operating room doing their routine tasks. They put away the laundry, check supplies, and put away the instruments, trying to finish in time for the pre-game show. Surely the doctors would want to stay home and watch the super bowl today!

"Work is all done Jenny, you grab the cokes and I'll pop the popcorn." Libby said as she flung a bag of popcorn into the microwave in the surgeon's lounge. On Sundays when there were no surgeons around, the nurses relaxed in their lounge as it was more comfortable and had a nice television in it.

"Leaded or unleaded?" Jenny asked referring to diet or regular coke.

"Unleaded."

"Ah, this is great! We finished up just in time to relax and enjoy the super bowl hype." Jenny said.

"I hope our luck holds out through the game. Could we be that fortunate?" Libby barely got the words from her mouth when the phone rang.

"Surgery, Libby James speaking. How may I help you?"

"Hi Libby, Sam Watters, I have a case to do." Dr. Watters was an informal kind of guy, about the same age as the two of them and he preferred to be called by his first name.

"Now?" Libby asked.

"Yes, why are you already doing a case?" He asked.

"No, we were planning on watching the super bowl, guess we aren't now."

"Sorry girls." Sam said. "Let's do a Total Hip instead for the fun of it."

"Ok. So, you are pulling our leg, right?" Libby asked. "You do realize that it is Sunday and we aren't staffed to do a total hip. There are only two of us here today." Libby was hoping he would change his mind.

"I know, but it has to be done today. And Libby, I want to use the new system. Ask Jenny if she is familiar with it."

"*Well I haven't used it.* I'll ask Jen if she has." Libby covered the phone with her hand. "Sam wants to do a Total Hip Replacement today and use the new system, are you familiar with it?"

"I have seen it, but never used it! There is a big difference! Is he nuts? Since when did a total hip become an emergency case?"

"Since we are so busy he can't get it scheduled through the week more than likely." Libby answered.

"Sam, Jenny hasn't used it but she knows what it looks like."

"We will be fine. The sales rep from the company is coming to help us. He can talk us through the equipment if there is a problem. Heck, I haven't used it either!" He said. "And for the record, I understand this isn't a normal kind of weekend case. I'll make it as easy on you as I can. Is there anything you need? Anything I can do to help you get read?" Aside from being a good surgeon, Sam was also a nice guy and his offer was genuine.

"If you could bring the patient down with you when you come, that would help. It would save us time from running to the floor to pick her up. Besides, Jenny is going to need all the time she can get to set up." Libby said.

"Fair enough, see you in about forty minutes." Sam replied.

Jenny was grateful that if they had to do a case like this on a Sunday afternoon that at least it was with Dr. Sam Watters. He was the easiest surgeons to work with and easy on the eyes aw sell. He had the biggest set of baby blue eyes she'd ever seen. When all you can see of a person in the operating room is their eyes, you learn to read them pretty well. Just like Grandpa Jake use to say, a person could talk with their eyes.

Jenny dialed the phone while Libby was still on the other line talking to Sam. She had to order the case cart from the Central Supply Department. It would contain the needed basic instruments, sponges and supplies for the surgery. Normally they couldn't even start to prepare the room without the case cart, but it would take some time for Central Supply to pull it together. Time they didn't have today, and in this case most of what they needed they already had on hand in the Total Joint Room right here in the department.

"Grab a custom Total Hip pack out of the workroom, we can start opening up the sterile supplies on it. Besides, using the custom pack will save us time because so much of what we already need is in it." Libby said. "We shouldn't even have to put out sponges or knife blades if we use the custom pack that CLS supplies for us."

The custom total hip pack was a specialty packaged unit they ordered from CLS supplies. It was designed to fit the needs of their orthopedic surgeons at Community General. They made other custom packs as well for other hospitals and other departments. Because of the diversified materials in the packs it was necessary to use gas sterilization instead of steam to insure complete sterilization of all the items in the pack. The prepared packs even contained the gowns and gloves to be used.

They heard the door to the surgical department open up, it was Dr. Watters with their patient. Dr. Romine, the anesthesiologist was with him.

David, the sales rep from the instrument company had arrived as well. He brought with him even more instruments and supplies. Jenny thought to herself that if she were any shorter she would need a ladder to see the over the top of the stack of instrument pans she had on her table. She fastened the oxygen helmet on her head and began to scrub her arms.

All total joint cases required what everyone referred to as their 'space suite'. A full helmet to cover the face and an oxygen tank strapped around your waist to vent in oxygen was used. When everything was hooked up you looked more like an astronaut than a doctor or nurse.

"What else can I get for you before I go talk to the patient? Libby asked Jenny.

"How about the kitchen sink, I seem to have forgotten it." She replied from behind the stack of metal trays filled with instruments. "Seriously though, if you can just stall and give me a few extra minutes to sort through this mess that would help. Besides, I need David to show me how to put these specialty instruments together. I don't have a clue."

"I'll get you hooked up to the oxygen pack so you can breathe and then I'll stall a few before I bring the patient in. I'll try to give you at least fifteen minutes." Libby said.

"Ok, that should be fine." Jenny knew she would have some time to set up while they positioned the patient and completed the necessary preparations.

Jenny's mind raced as she scurried around the room, picking through the pans of instruments, taking only what she was certain she needed from each tray. She felt weird, she shook off the feeling. She didn't have time for 'weird' right now. Besides, it was probably just nerves. Who in their right mind wouldn't be a bit nervous about doing a case of this magnitude on a Sunday afternoon! Under normal circumstances when a total hip was done, it required two circulating nurses, two scrub nurses and two surgeons with their two assistants and of course the anesthesiologist. That was a total of nine people that it normally took to do a case such as this. Today, it was just the anesthesiologist, Libby and Jenny with Dr. Watters. Oh, and we mustn't forget David, the sales rep! While Jenny had nerves of steel in the operating room under most circumstances, this was a bit unusual. Not the 'patient may not make it' kind of scenario, but the overwhelmed with instruments kind of scenario. Yes, she was sure the 'weird' feeling she had must have been nerves.

The case got underway and David was talking in her ear constantly as he explained each instrument and how to assemble it. While Sam was an excellent surgeon today he reminded her of a little boy with a new toy as he played with the new equipment.

"It is so hot in here!" Jenny said as she looked at Libby. "Is it just me?"

"I think it is you Jenny, you don't look very good." Libby replied as she herself wore two jackets and had a warm blanket around her shoulders. But she could clearly see that Jenny's face was beat red. "I think you are just getting old." She joked.

"Thanks a lot!" She teased. "Careful, we are the same age, remember?"

"You really don't look good Jenny; do you want us to call in the backup scrub?" Sam asked.

"No, I'm fine, but you just broke my heart by telling me I didn't look good!" She was trying hard to lighten the mood. Jenny hated for people to fuss over her, but wow, she was starting to feel really sick. Her wrists and forearms felt as if someone were holding a match to them and her eyes were so dry she could barely blink. She felt nauseated and had developed a splitting headache.

"Shake it off Jenny." She said to herself. No time for this right now.

Libby turned the thermostat down even lower and picked up blankets out of the warmer for her and Dr. Romine.

Jenny started saying a Psalms in her head: "They that wait upon the Lord, He shall renew their strength, they shall mount up with wings as eagles. They shall run and not be weary; they shall walk and not faint. Teach me Lord; teach me Lord, to wait."

She was truly hoping for that 'not faint' part to hold true. She felt as if she could drop at any second.

Four hours later, the case was finished. Sam thanked them for their help and told them they had done a great job. Jenny could not wait to get out of the space suit! She pulled off her helmet the oxygen tank off her waist. She had been in that gown for over five hours! When she pulled it off she noticed her arms were extremely red and hot with little water blisters all over her forearms from her wrist upward onto her forearm about five inches.

"Wow, what a little stress can do to you." She thought to herself. She didn't give it another thought. They still had work to do. Most of the dirty instruments could be sent back downstairs in an empty case cart to Central Supply to be cleaned. But many of the instruments stayed in their department and had to be washed, sterilized and taken back to the total joint room. They bagged up the trash, mopped the floor and talked about the case as they worked.

"You didn't look so good for a while in there Jenny, I thought you were going to faint on me. Are you feeling better?" Libby asked as they cleaned up.

"I know, I felt pretty strange for a while. I guess I was just stressed. It was a bit nerve racking not knowing the instruments. Who ever heard of doing a total hip on a Sunday?"

"I think we need a break." Libby suggested as they made their way back to the doctors lounge. When they got there a pizza waited for them on the table with a note from Dr. Watters.

"Sorry I ruined your super bowl Sunday plans girls! Great job though and thanks!" Signed; "Sam".

They were hungry. Jenny didn't eat much though, she felt nauseated.

Unaware of it then, but that was the beginning of the end of her career as a Surgical Technologist. That day changed her life forever. Her faith was about to be shaken to the core, and her marriage to the limit.

Chapter Seven

It must be true that when you get close to forty you begin to fall apart. Jenny hadn't felt good since that day in January when she did the case on Super Bowl Sunday with Dr. Watters. She was always exhausted and an unusual rash remained on her arms constantly. If she ever thought she had a headache before, she had been wrong. She now experienced full out and out migraines complete with the nausea and vomiting. Blurred vision, dizzy spells, insomnia and feeling 'disconnected' from the world were daily experiences for her now. Is it possible that this was all from stress? She did work long hours and Rob had started his own business just a year ago. Being a self-employed Farrier, he traveled all over the country shoeing horses and making horseshoes. It was what he loved. It took him away from his family, but it made him happy. Maybe, that is what made him happy, being away from his family. Their marriage was hitting the rocks and Jenny had no idea how to stop it. It was like a freight train out of control. Rob had an affair several years back, but Jenny had forgiven him. They had gotten married so young and she kind of expected it sooner or later. That didn't make it hurt any less. She loved Rob with all her heart and was determined to fight for her marriage. She had completely forgiven him as God would expect her to do. Forgive and forget. Jenny didn't believe in divorce. Her parents had been divorced and so had Robs. She was determined not to put her sons through that. But on their way to Florida a few weeks ago to visit Rob's uncle, he told her he wanted a legal separation. She was convinced her lack of energy and poor health was stress related. How could it not be?

Lisa and Jenny were sharing a scrub sink on a busy morning in March. They were comparing their assignments for the day. Sometimes they traded surgeons or cases if one of them had a doctor that she didn't work well with.

"Ouch, I wish this rash would go away!" Jenny said as she scrubbed over her now raw arms. "It really hurts to scrub it."

"What rash?" Lisa asked, as she glanced at Jenny's arms. "Jenny, that looks like the same rash that Linda and Jamie had. Didn't you see their arms? It was just a couple of weeks ago they both broke out with a rash just like that one. There was a notice on the bulletin board in the lounge about it"

"What notice? I've been on vacation for two weeks with Rob in Florida, remember?" Jenny reminded her friend.

"There was a posting about not wearing any gowns from the custom packs because of a possible connection to the rash that Jamie and Linda had." Lisa said. "Jenny, you better get your arms looked at. I'm not kidding, it looks the same. I guess they were doing a total hip one day when they noticed their arms itching and they burned. When the case was over they had this rash and it looked just like yours." Lisa was studying Jenny's arms. "I'm serious Jen; you better break scrub and let Katie take a look at your arms."

"I don't think so! It is just nerves, you know how stressed I've been with the situation with Rob lately."

"That does it good buddy!" Lisa said as she stopped scrubbing instead. "If you won't take care of yourself, I will just have to do it for you! I'm going to get Katie."

A few minutes later, Lisa returned with Katie in tow. Katie was the nurse supervisor over the orthopedic department. Concern was written all over Katie's face as she examined Jenny's arms.

"How long have you had this rash Jenny?" She asked.

"Off and on since January." Jenny replied. "It's nothing, just stress."

"It *is something*, why didn't you report it?"

"It's just a rash Katie. I've had it since super bowl Sunday." Jenny pulled her arms away from Katie, who hadn't stopped rubbing them the whole time they talked.

"Why is it you remember the 'exact' day you got the rash?" Katie asked her.

"Because Libby and I were doing a case with Dr. Watters, a total hip, and after that my rash appeared. I assumed it was just nerves."

"You know better than to 'assume' anything Jenny. It just makes an 'ass' out of 'you' and 'me.' You know, ASS-U-ME. I want you to go to the employee health department and see Sandi Martin now." Katie said in a stern voice. "Jenny, did you and Libby use a custom pack that day?"

"Yes, of course we did."

"Have you since?" She asked.

"Sure, every time I do an Arthroscope." Jenny replied.

"Go see Sandi. I'll get someone else to scrub your case." The tone in her voice convinced Jenny to not argue with her.

Jenny walked into Sandi's office, Katie had already called her and she was expected. She had to go through the whole story again of when she first noticed the rash. Looking at Jenny's arms, Sandi started shaking her head.

"I want you to go to Kim Hanner's office. She is the supervisor for Central Supply, you know Kim don't you?" Sandi asked. "Your rash is identical to the other four girls I have seen this month."

"Four? I thought there were just two. What does Kim have to do with this?"

"It is possible the rash is connected to the gowns that are packaged in the custom packs we receive from the CLS surgical supply company." Sandi said.

Jenny thought about what Sandi said as she walked down to Central Supply. It did make sense. She had been bothered off and on by this rash since January, after the weekend total hip. Constantly continuing to scrub her arms raw and wearing other gowns from CLS had only made it worse. Jenny was rarely sick a day in her life and preferred not to make a big deal out of a little rash. But it was more than a little rash; she had been feeling horrible since January.

Once inside Kim's office she listened as she was told about a possible exposure to the chemicals; Ethylene Oxide and the derivative, Ethylene Chlorohydrin. It seems there may be chemical residue in the cuffs of the surgical gowns. They are not being properly aerated out of the packs. When worn by the scrub nurses, the chemicals are then being absorbed into their systems through their skin.

"Jenny, would you mind if I have the hospital photographer take photos of your arms." Kim asked. "It is much more evident on your arms than on the others that the rash is in the direct area of the gown cuffs."

"No problem." Jenny was stunned. *Chemicals, exposures, what was going on here?*

The photographer took several photos of her arms. All the time he was shaking his head as he muddled under his breath about how *amazing* this was. When he was done, Kim came back into the room.

"I'll keep you posted on any news about this Jenny. Meanwhile, I want you to use the Liodex ointment that Sandi gave you. She did give you some didn't she?" Kim asked.

"Ah, yes, I think so. Yes, she did." Jenny walked out of Kim's office in a complete daze. What in the world had just happened?

Rob had been out of town working. Jenny sat by the phone waiting on him to call that night. They had not yet separated as Rob's uncle had passed away. They hadn't even talked any more about it. She needed him now so much. Finally, he called.

"Hello." Jenny picked up the receiver.

"Hi. How is everything there?" Always his first question as he always wanted to know how the horses were doing and the boys. He wasn't prepared at all for her response.

Just hearing his voice sat Jenny off onto a crying spree. She couldn't seem to stop and she was sobbing so hard, Rob couldn't make any sense out of a word she said.

"Jenny, slow down. What's wrong, are the boys ok? Did something happen to one of the horses?" He asked as she continued to cry. "Dammit Jenny! Stop crying and tell me what is going on!" He was getting worried.

"I'm sorry Rob. The boys are fine and so are the horses." She sniffed. "I just really need to talk to you; I have to tell you something."

Rob was silent on the other end of the phone as he listened to her tell him about the events of the day. When she finished, he didn't speak.

"Rob, are you still there? Did you hear what I just said?"

"I heard." He finally said. "I'm twelve hours from home and you have to spring something like this on me? You couldn't wait until I came home to tell me this? You aren't even sure of what is really going on yet are you?" Rob snapped angrily at her.

"No, but we are having a meeting with the hospital administration next week so they can tell us more." Jenny quietly said.

"So, basically, you are telling me you have a rash. You don't know why but it may be from a chemical. You are crying out of control because of that?" He was being very snippy with her. "Why didn't you just wait until you knew for sure what was going on before you get upset and call me to get me worked up when I'm out trying to make a living for us?"

"I just needed to talk to you Rob." She felt so hurt. "Maybe I jumped to conclusions, I was just scared Rob. I'm sorry."

"I'll see you when I get home. Give the boys my love." He hung up the phone.

These days it was always; "Give the boys my love." Never, "I love you Jenny." She couldn't remember the last time he had said those words to her.

"God, what is happening to me?" Jenny thought. She prayed, but her fear and anger was standing directly between her and her God. She wondered if her prayers were even being heard now.

Chapter Eight

The months that followed brought with them the constant change of events. Rumors ran unabated like a river to the sea about the 'rash' that was spreading in their department. By the end of April they had at least a few answers when a 'right to know' meeting was called. Present at the meeting were:

Katie Pogue, R.N.-Nurse Supervisor over Orthopedics.

Linda Peters, R.N.-effected staff member.

Jamie Baker, R.N.-effected staff member.

Jill Mason, R.N.-effected staff member.

Kim Hanner, R.N. - Nurse Supervisor over Central Supply.

Melissa Townsend, C.S.T.-effected staff member.

Jenny Reed, C.S.T.-effected staff member.

Lisa Hoover, C.S.T. - effected staff member.

Dennis Oakley, Director of Clinical Engineering.

Jim Olsen, C.E.O of Community General.

It was official. Testing had been done on the chemical level of Ethylene Oxide and Ethylene Chlorohydrin residue in the gowns. The report was far higher than the recommended safety levels allowed by OSHA.

The next six months were a constant blur of headaches, nausea, skin rashes and vision problems. When the dust settled, there were six registered nurses and six surgical technologists exposed to the chemicals.

By May, the hospital administrators had begun meetings with all twelve effected staff personnel and a representative from the CLS Company. A regional manager and vice president were present on their behalf at all of the meetings.

They discussed the different methods used to extract the chemicals from the cuffs of the gowns to measure the residual levels. Individual sterilizers, size and design were all contributing factors. It all became so 'technical' and complex to them.

Kim had reported the Ethylene Chlorohydrin level was their main concern. It was as high as 300-400 parts per million (PPM). Far above the OSHA standard for safety that was a low 5PPM.

Bob Masters, Vice President of CLS admitted they were aware of a problem in the past regarding the gown cuffs, going back to December of 1990. He reported that routine monitoring was only done on the standard packs and not the custom packs. He also reported that routine monitoring wasn't even done on the 'specialty' ordered packs. Mr. Masters went on to state that while he did not know for certain that the skin irritations reported by the hospital employees was due to unduly high chemical levels, he was aware that his company had exceeded the safety limits. He assured us that the problem would be resolved.

Mr. Masters offered medical advice on the long term side effects of Ethylene Oxide (EO) and Ethylene Chlorohydrin (EC). Plans had been made for Dr. James Keller to come to Community General and speak with those involved. A list of questions and concerns were made to present to Dr. Keller. He requested that a routine CBC, Chem 12 and urinalysis be done prior to his arrival on each of the effected staff members. He would from CSL headquarters in Utah to spend a day in conference with the staff and administration to answer questions.

By the end of May, they had all sat through hours after hours of meetings. CSL had invited all of them to tour their sterilization facility in Mexico, all expenses paid of course. Their invitation was declined, unanimously.

The May 28th meeting with Dr. Keller proved to be the most interesting and yet frightening meeting. During the mid-morning session it was noted that although Dr. Keller was 'familiar' with EO exposures, he knew little about EC exposures.

Dr. Keller began the afternoon session with an apology.

"First, I would like to apologize for coming to your hospital with insufficient knowledge to help you. My field of experience has been strictly with employees exposed to EO gas, by inhalation. Your exposure to both EO and EC, through skin absorption is quite different. It seems obvious to me that you need to address someone other than myself."

"Dr. Keller, I understand that you don't feel completely qualified to help us." Jenny spoke up. "But, in your professional opinion, is EC a potentially more dangerous substance than EO?"

"I can't refute that right now Mrs. Reed, because of the type of exposure. Skin absorption is different than strictly inhalation." Dr. Keller continued. "I can say that the level of EC you were exposed to was high enough to cause concern regarding systemic toxic exposure. It was indeed, overwhelmingly high. I am not aware however of a good human study on known exposure to Ethylene Chlorohydrin."

Why has it taking so long for CLS to get information together for us about the chemicals? And why did they send someone whom they knew couldn't answer all of our questions." Linda asked.

"I can't answer that." Dr. Keller replied. "I can tell you, these levels are highly unacceptable."

They looked like zombies as they walked out of the meeting. Here was a doctor that CLS had sent to 'answer' questions and to put them at ease regarding their exposure, but now they had even more questions than before. Dr. Keller had only fueled their fears, not put them to ease. They had not heard one thing to give them comfort. They had hoped to hear that it was a mistake, no exposure had happened. Instead, they heard words like; "overwhelming unacceptable levels."

The group later gathered at the local McDonalds for a private meeting of their own, trying to put things into perspective. Although a good stiff margarita sounded better, they settled for French fries and a shake.

"I think we are in deep crap." Linda said.

All of them agreed. It was as if the river was rising and their boat had a hole in it and no one was throwing them a life raft.

"What do we do now?" Jill, usually the quiet one, was near panic. "Did any of you read the reports from Sweden that they handed out on EC exposure? That is one SERIOUS chemical!"

"I read a little of it." Jamie said. "Wish I hadn't. It can cause brain cancer, leukemia, central nervous system disorders, visual problems and more."

"The list of potential side effects was a mile long. And did you notice that all the reports were based on POST MORTUM studies!?" Lisa whispered. "Our chance of surviving this without any systemic disease looks pretty slim!"

"I know one thing for sure. They can keep their free trip to Mexico!" Melissa said.

"I think we better speak to a lawyer, this is getting over our heads." Jenny finally said what they were all thinking. "Agreed?"

They all agreed.

"Well, my fellow 'rash-rats'. I have to get home. I will do some research on attorneys and you guys do the same. Let me know if you have any suggestions." Jenny said.

"Rash-rats." Linda mumbled. "It does seem to fit us."

The nickname stuck.

Chapter Nine

Jenny popped her knuckles nervously as she sat across from Rob at the kitchen table.

"What time is he coming?" He asked.

"In about an hour, I hope he doesn't have any trouble finding our house."

"How many of the others do you think will show up?"

"Everyone, at least they all said they could make it." Jenny answered.

A friend had told Jenny about the legal firm of "Newman and Chapel". They had heard one of their attorney's give a lecture on patient rights at a seminar. They knew they didn't want a local attorney. This was too big a case for someone local to handle. So Jenny called the firm from Detroit. She explained their need for legal advice after a chemical exposure. One of the senior partners, Mr. Stevens, was coming to talk with them this afternoon. He had suggested that since there were twelve of them and only one of him, he would come to them.

Lisa was the first to arrive, mostly to give Jenny help with the refreshments. Rob decided he would go out to his shop in the barn. He needed to get some horseshoes turned for some of his clients and he didn't want to be in the house when the meeting started.

The rest of the group began to arrive, as did Mr. Stevens. Once everyone was there and they had made their introductions, each of them was asked by Mr. Stevens, to describe in their own words what had happened. He took notes and listened intently. They told him the medical symptoms they had been experience. They described the nausea, fatigue, visual problems, memory loss, urinary tract infections, muscle weakness and more.

Mr. Stevens asked them a lot of questions regarding the initial rash on their arms. He wanted to know about their sensitivity to sun, and the recurrent contact dermatitis they experienced.

After approximately two hours of discussion, he gave them an answer to their question.

"Yes, you most definitely need an attorney." He stated. "You have a case, a damn good one from what I can see. The firm I work for has a long standing rule. We don't take cases we don't feel we can win." He continued. "I'm going to let you girls talk this over. If you decided you want to pursue your options in this matter, I will take your case. You can call me when you are ready."

After Mr. Stevens left they spent the next few hours in their own discussion. Rehashing what he had said to them and tossing around the pro's and cons of accepting legal his council. They took a vote, it was unanimous. Jenny would call Mr. Stevens first thing in the morning and tell him, he had twelve new clients; the rash rats.

Community General put on a good front of being concerned for their employee's health and welfare. They had hopes that a 'joint' lawsuit could be filed against CLS. However when they discovered that the girls had hired their own attorney, to say things got 'intense' at work was an understatement.

Outwardly the higher administration displayed an appearance of total cooperation with Mr. Stevens. Inwardly, nurse supervisors as well as some of the other staff and surgeons, were giving them as much antagonism as possible. They were often referred to as 'the gold diggers' or the 'trouble makers' by some. For the most part, they had the support of the people they worked with most often. Those that saw firsthand the effect that the chemical had on them, were supportive. But still, it was hard to overlook the snide remarks of others. They found out who their friends were and which doctors were compassionate, as well as which ones were downright cruel.

Many of the 'rash rats' had developed some sensitivity on their wrists. Jenny's seemed to be worse. She could no longer tolerate the disposable gowns. The chloride in the bleached cuffs of the gowns irritated her already sensitive skin. Anything at all tight around her wrist was very uncomfortable. Wearing a watch was even uncomfortable. Her dermatologist had specifically written a note to the hospital that she was not to wear disposable gowns for any reason. Contact dermatitis was always the result of wearing a gown sterilized by chemicals. Recently, the hospital had switched from the regular cloth surgical gowns to a more water resilient nylon gown. There was no reason for forcing anyone to wear the disposable gowns any longer as the nylon ones were just as water resistant.

Jenny noticed that she was doing more and more orthopedic cases, not that she minded, she loved ortho cases. However it was expected that you were to wear disposable gowns on any and all ortho cases. Jenny had been substituting the new nylon gowns instead. She had been wearing the nylon for over four months and no one had complained. Not until now.

Dr. Peck had a real knack for stirring up trouble, and his nurse, Cheri, didn't mind rocking the boat either and did so every chance she got. Jenny was assigned to Dr. Peck's room to do a Compression Hip Screw case. Cheri approached her and whispered in her ear.

"You will need to put on a disposable paper gown." She told Jenny.

"What?" Jenny thought she had heard Cheri wrong because everyone knew that Jenny's doctors had told her not to. None of the other surgeons had insisted she change out of her nylon gown. They were all aware the integrity of the nylon gowns was just as good, if not better than the paper gowns.

"I SAID," Cheri repeated with a hint of pleasure in her voice, "put on a paper gown."

"I can't and you know it." Jenny said calmly. "I am under Doctors care and the paper gowns irritate my arms, and make the dermatitis flair up."

"I'm afraid you have to. Dr. Peck INSISTS. If you are going to be in HIS room, working HIS case, you will wear the gown HE wants you to wear." Cheri said rudely.

The last thing Jenny wanted was to get into a debate with Cheri.

"Linda," Jenny said as she turned to her circulating nurse. "Get Katie for me, now."

It was obvious to Linda what was going on here, after all she too, was a 'rash rat'. Lind had been forced to give up scrubbing all together because of the dermatitis from the exposure. Jenny didn't have that choice. She was a C.S.T. at Community General. And C.S.T.'s scrubbed or they didn't work. Linda was an R.N. She could circulate the case and not have to scrub if she chose not to. But for Jenny, her job, was scrubbing.

When Katie came into the room she pretended not to know what was going on.

"What do you need Jenny?" She asked.

"We seem to have a problem here." Jenny replied. "Dr. Peck is insisting I wear a paper gown. You and I both know that I can't do that. Would you talk to him?"

"I'll see what I can do." Katie said as she left the room to speak to him. Dr. Peck was standing right outside the room in the scrub area, visible to Jenny through the window above the scrub sink. She could tell the conversation wasn't taking a good turn.

81

Katie was a little condescending when she came back into the room.

"Jenny, if you would just put on a disposable gown over top of your nylon one, he will be content."

"I have on a twenty-pound lead apron because we are going to be doing X-rays in the procedure, and my nylon gown. Are you saying you want me to put on yet another gown over top of these?" Jenny was amazed at how stupid this all seemed. "Do you have any idea how hot that would be? No, I won't do that. I'd pass out from the heat." Jenny said. "Can't you find anyone to switch cases with me?"

"I'll try, I don't think I can." Katie said, leaving the room. "But I will try."

Katie stopped in the scrub area again, speaking to Dr. Peck.

A few minutes later, she returned.

"I'm sorry Jenny, there just isn't anyone available." Katie said. "And Dr. Peck still insists you change your gown, and I have to back him up."

Was this the same Kati Pogue who just a few months ago had been so 'concerned' about her rash? Katie scrubbed too, but was she offering to relieve Jenny? No, she wasn't. She was standing behind the good doctor. Good doctor indeed, that is a joke, Jenny thought.

Jenny was absolutely being pushed into a corner. They were forcing her to do something she didn't want to do. Refusing a direct order from her nurse supervisor was insubordination. You could be fired for that, and they knew it.

Insubordination wasn't her style, but they were toying with her health. No one else was going to stand up for her, she would do it herself.

"I'm not putting on that paper gown Katie. You can write me up or fire me, do whatever you have to do. But I will NOT, understand? I will NOT wear a paper gown!" Jenny meant it. She held her head hey and looked Katie straight in the eye. "You go tell Dr. Peck, if he doesn't want me in HIS room, as I am, he and Cheri can do this case alone!"

If there had been any danger of her actions affecting the patient's welfare, Jenny would never have pushed the issue. She would have risked her own life first. But this was a 'compression screw'. In the past, Jenny had done many such cases with just herself and the surgeon. Cheri and Dr. Peck had done them without the assistance of a scrub nurse before. They could do it alone easily. If she could do a total hip replacement with just herself and Dr. Watters, they could surely handle this case alone.

Katie stepped back into the scrub area and spoke to Dr. Peck. He wasn't happy. She returned to the room.

"Do this case, and report to my office immediately after." Katie said to her.

Jenny felt almost a twinge of sympathy for Katie. She had been put in the middle of his little power play. Any respect Jenny may have had for Dr. Peck, was long gone. Any man who couldn't come into the room and speak for himself directly was a whimp! He hid behind his own nurse and Jenny's supervisor.

There room was extremely quiet during the case as Jenny did her job and Dr. Peck did his. It took nearly two hours and Jenny had a sore on her lip from biting it to keep from speaking her mind to the 'so called man'.

Katie must have been a real social butterfly during those two hours. As Jenny walked down the hallway to Katie's office, she could feel the eyes on her. The whispers behind her back were obvious too. Staff members questioned her about what had happened in her room. They were talking about the 'big conference' that had been called. Jenny was the topic of conversation.

She knocked on the door of Katie's office.

"Come in." Katie said. "Pull up a chair and sit down, if you can find one."

Katie had indeed been a busy girl, her office was filled. Pam Easton, the director of surgical services. Barbara Larson, nurse supervisor of the operating room, and Larry Michaelson, hospital epidemiologist all joined her in her tiny office.

"I have discussed our little problem with the rest of the group here." Katie began. "It has always been our

84

policy at Community General that a disposable gown is worn on any orthopedic case."

"We can't let one scrub nurse break that rule, while others must abide by it." Barbara said. "We can try to keep you out of orthopedics as much as possible, but with you working a twelve hour shift, that won't be totally possible."

"Excuse me." Jenny interrupted. "You said that this was hospital policy? I want to see the policy. I'd like to read it myself."

"Well, it isn't a written policy. It has just always been an unspoken rule." Barbara said.

"I beg your pardon." Jenny was not intimidated by their little 'show of force'. "I have learned a little something from my six-years on national committees for surgical technology. One little tidbit I picked up was; IF it isn't a WRITTEN policy, it is NOT a policy. It has to be 'written' to be official."

"Larry," Jenny continued, "the reasoning behind disposable gowns is that they are used because they are water repellent, is that not true?"

"That is the theory." Larry had to admire Jenny's spunk. She was normally a quiet, non-argumentative person. Backed into a corner and out comes a wildcat!

"It is true that the old cotton gowns we used were not water repellent. They offered little protection to us against blood and body fluids, and gave little protection to the patient against germs. But our new nylon gowns are.

85

They are even more water repellent than the paper gowns."
Jenny stated. "That being true, it shouldn't matter if I wear
paper or nylon, as long as they are impervious and don't
allow body fluids or water to pass through. Should it?"

"No, it shouldn't." Larry began to ramble. "But I
don't have any reports on the nylon gowns, or any statistics
from quality assurance."

Jenny interrupted him. "This is how it stands. I
have a doctor at University Hospital that says I cannot wear
paper gowns." Jenny was not about to back down. "IF you
have a problem with that, take it up with my attorney. You
all know Mr. Stevens. Talk to him. Until HE tells me not
to, I will follow my doctor's advice. I will NOT wear the
paper gowns!"

As she walked out of the meeting and slammed the
door behind her, Jenny felt a lot like 'Little Sister" in the
John Wayne movie, "Rooster Cogburn". Little Sister was
constantly threatening people with her 'Lawyer Tackett".
When pushed to the limit, Jenny could be a force not to be
reckoned with.

Sleep did not come to her that night. The more she
thought about the events that had taken place that day, the
more frustrated she became. By morning she had worked
her way up to a blazing anger. She was tired. She was tired
of the 'rash-rats', tired of being the topic of gossip in the
operating lounge and the operating room. She was tired of
the hush that would fall over a room whenever she or one
of the others would walk in. She was so very tired of the
snide remarks about how they were too 'good' to follow the

rules. People thought they were getting special treatment, because 'maybe' they had been exposed to some stupid chemical. Jenny was just plain tired!

Putting on a white lab coat, Jenny grabbed a nylon gown and started out of the department.

"Hey, where are you going in such a hurry?" Lisa's voice echoed down the hall. "You look like you're going to a fire!"

"I am." Jenny answered.

"What?"

"Well, I'm probably going to 'get' fired." Jenny responded. "You better stay here or you may get fired too!"

"Well, that's ok. As long as I know what I'm getting fired for. Now what are we doing and where are we going?" Lisa laughed.

"You'll see."

"Seriously, if I'm going to get fired, don't you think you should at least tell me why?" Lisa said. "Now, for the last time, where are WE going?"

"Larry Michaelson's office." Jenny answered.

"OH CRAP!" Lisa was stunned. Now she knew they may really get fired.

But Lisa stayed beside her friend. Jenny was really upset and friends don't let friends stand alone. If Jenny was going down, Jenny was going with her.

Jenny didn't even knock. She just opened the door to Larry's office and walked in.

"Larry Michelson, I want to talk to you."

Larry nearly fell out of the chair he had been sitting in with his feet propped up on his desk as they barged in.

"Jenny, Lisa, hello." He greeted them as casually as if it were a social visit. Although he could tell, it was anything but that. "How are you ladies this morning?"

Not even acknowledging his greeting, Jenny got down to business.

"IF I can prove to you that these nylon gowns are impervious, beyond any shadow of a doubt will you back up my right to wear them instead of the paper ones? Jenny asked.

"If they really are Jenny, I will do all I can." Larry said.

That was all Jenny needed to hear. She trusted Larry, he was a fair man. She almost felt bad about what she was going to do next. She opened up the nylon gown on top of Larry's desk. His morning paper along with mounds of paper work was piled underneath the gown. Larry looked it over, checking the threads and the material.

"Sure feels impervious, but that doesn't mean it really is."

AS Jenny glanced around the room she saw Larry's morning coffee on the corner of his desk.

"Do you have any more coffee" Jenny asked.

"Sure, I'll get you a cup." Larry started to rise from his seat.

"That won't be necessary." She said as she quickly grabbed his coffee cup and dumped the contents of it in the center of the nylon gown. "But you may want to get you another cup."

Larry's eyes were as big as silver dollars. Jenny had just dumped a whole cup of hot coffee on top of the gown on his desk! If it soaked through, everything underneath it would be ruined! His morning paper and his quality assurance reports!

Lisa's lower jaw almost hit the floor as she watched in total shock, what Jenny had done.

"Relax Larry, the gown is water repellant." Jenny said as she picked the gown up by the corners. The coffee beaded up and rolled off of it into the trash can, leaving the gown and Larry's desk, perfectly dry. "See, impervious, just as I said it was. Now, do we have a deal or not?

"We do." Larry was stunned. "And I will contact the orthopedic surgeons association myself and request their policies on the nylon gowns."

"That's all I can expect, thank you Larry." Jenny said.

As she and Lisa were walking out his door, Larry said; "Jenny, next time? Bring your own damn coffee!" He smiled.

Two weeks later, Jenny received a message to stop by Larry's office

"Come on in Jenny. I have some news." He said. "Congratulations, you can wear your nylon gowns in any case you choose. Orthopedic included."

"Has Dr. Peck been informed of this?" Jenny asked.

"He certainly has and he was none too happy about it."

"Thanks Larry, really, I appreciate your support."

Jenny left his office with a sense of victory, however small. She had won the battle, but the war raged on.

Chapter Ten

Mr. Stevens called a meeting with his clients and the hospital administration early in September, approximately seven months after the exposures began.

Community General had agreed to let workman's compensation cover all the medical expenses that the nursing staff were accumulating due to their exposure to the chemicals. It wasn't that they really had their best interest at heart. They just didn't want to be named in their lawsuit also. CLS didn't shoulder all the responsibility, it also fell upon Community General's own quality assurance personnel that had dropped the ball.

Mr. Stevens had arranged for a team of doctors from State University Medical Center to examine the nurses and techs. Each of them had been given a list of specialist they were to see:

A Neurologist: to assess the extent of the damage to their central nervous system.

A Psychologist: To evaluate their mental state due to all of the trauma and stress they were going through.

A Dermatologist: To follow their recurrent contact dermatitis and the rash on their arms. Jenny had been seeing the dermatologist for several months already.

A Pulmonary Specialist: To evaluate damage to their lungs.

An Ophthalmologist: Nearly all of them had experienced some kind of visual problems.

A Rheumatologist: Joint pain was also a common complaint.

An Endocrinologist: Could their glands have been affected?

An Urologist: Kidney and bladder problems had surfaced.

A Hematologist: Lab tests for signs of early leukemia were necessary every six months or so.

And the list would grow and grow….

Jenny had been having problems with her vision. In the past she had needed glasses only for a mild stigmatism as a child. She seldom needed them as an adult, only when she had eyestrain from sewing or reading too much. In May, four months after the exposure she saw her ophthalmologist. Her vision had changed drastically. She now needed bifocals and her eyes were exceptionally dry and focus was poor.

When at work under the florescent lighting and the spotlights in the operating room she often developed migraines. It was necessary to use eye drops several times a day.

Jenny was scrubbed in on a routine breast biopsy with one of her favorite surgeons, Dr. Derkin. Though her vision had been blurry all day, she had grown accustom to it and continued to scrub. It seemed like her vision was blurry every day anymore and she had decided to just ignore it and keep working. Today though, it felt as if she were on the outside of the world looking in. As Dr. Derkin began to close the wound, Jenny felt the room starting to fade away. Sounds and voices became magnified, and she felt as though she were looking through a veil of rain, then total darkness. No light, no vision, just extremely magnified sounds. She felt hot, yet cold to the bone.

"Sharon!" Jenny was hanging on to the operating table to keep from falling. "I need to sit down, NOW!"

The urgency in Jenny's voice brought Sharon instantly to her side. She grabbed Jenny's arm, contaminating her sterility immediately sitting her down on a stool. Jenny was pale and clammy.

"Are you ok? What's wrong?" Sharon questioned.

Jenny's normal easy going, polite attitude was gone.

"No, I am NOT ok. I can't see you!" There was fear in her voice.

Sharon quickly untied Jenny's gown and helped her to sit on the floor along the wall. She was afraid if Jenny fainted she would fall off the stool and she needed to leave the room for help. Sharon placed a cold, wet cloth on Jenny's forehead.

"Can you see me yet Jenny? Can you see anything at all?"

"No, and I feel really strange."

Dr. Derkin was finishing up his surgery. He broke scrub and immediately came to check on Jenny.

"You better get her to the lounge to lie down." He told Sharon after he looked into Jenny's eyes and felt her head.'

"Ok, just let me call for another circulating nurse for you first."

"I'll do that, you take care of Jen." He said.

"Ok." She helped Jenny to her feet. As they started walking down the hall, Jenny's vision started to return. It had only been gone a few minutes, but to Jenny it seemed like hours! It didn't come back clearly, but then, it hadn't been clear when she lost it. It was even more blurred and fuzzy, and she felt so very dizzy!

Barb Larson felt Jenny needed to be seen by her family doctor and since she couldn't drive obviously she would have the hospital security guards drive her. He waited for her while Dr. Ken Nelson examined her.

"I'm fine now Ken, really." Jenny peered into the bright light he held in front of her eyes.

Ken was not only Jen's doctor, but her best friend's brother as well. When Rob had started his own business and money was tight, Ken gave her a part time job in his office to help them make ends meet. He scheduled her hours in the office around her hours at the hospital.

"How long do you think you were without site?" Ken was still examining her eyes with his annoying light. "How long Jen?"

"One to four minutes probably." She mumbled. "I don't really know Ken, I couldn't SEE the clock."

"Not funny, this is serious." He said as he turned out the beacon he had been shinning into her eyes. "I want you to go see an Ophthalmologist, maybe at the University.

"I already have an appointment in a few weeks, with the chief of Ophthalmology there. Can it wait till then?"

"I suppose, it would probably be that long before we could get you in anyway, unless this happens again before then." He said. "And you WILL let me know if you have more problems before then, right?"

"I will."

"Now, I want you to get someone to drive you home and take the rest of the week off work. And get some rest Jenny. You aren't taking care of yourself." He said. "How are things at home? Is Rob handling this whole thing any better?"

"No, he isn't and things aren't going well at all." She answered him. "Ken, I don't want to talk about it ok?"

Denial, she was in denial, Ken thought to himself. Don't talk about it, don't deal with it, and maybe it will go away. He shook his head and gave her a hug.

"Go home, rest."

"Ok."

She walked around in a fog the next few weeks. Although she had not completely lost her vision again she was still experiencing a lot of blurred vision, almost a tunnel vision. She had had several follow up appointments with the Ophthalmologist and was going again in a few days, it was now already October.

She and Rob were going to take off for a long weekend and go to a horse show in Detroit. This trip was a yearly outing for them with the horses and she was really looking forward to getting away for a few days! It was going to be so wonderful. Time alone with Rob was just what she needed now. She was hoping to narrow the gap that had been widening between them. The distance between them had grown so huge that Jenny felt she could barely see him on the other side. They didn't talk much and they seldom saw each other! When they did see each other, Jenny talked about the case and Rob talked about horses and neither one of them really heard the other.

The day came for them to leave and Jenny felt awful, but she wasn't about to let Rob know. He would make her stay home and while this was 'vacation' to her, it was a 'working trip' for him. She wasn't about to miss this trip.

On Friday evening, Jenny was sitting in the stands at the Detroit horse show. She and some of the other wives of horsemen were catching up on the latest gossip. Jenny would much rather have been in the arena with Rob and the horses but lately, he didn't want her there. He would point to the stands and tell her to go sit down, like a father telling his child where to sit. And like a child, instead of a wife, Jenny obeyed.

Nothing exciting ever happened in the stands. The other women's chatter distracted her so much that she missed out on all that was happening in the arena with the horses and Rob. Sometimes she didn't even know who won the contest! When she was in the arena with Rob she was part of it all. Their Draft Horse team was always in the top five and a threat to win any Horse Pulling Competition they went to. She preferred to be down there with Rob, holding the horses and share in the victory, or defeat with him. She loved that, not sitting in the stands with the other wives. She was a horsewoman too, not just a bystander. With him being on the road so much of the time she was the one always taking care of the horses. But when he was home, he treated her like she knew nothing about them. Odd since she often felt he loved his horses more than her, so why would he trust her with them if he didn't feel she could take care of him just as well as he does?

But since Jenny felt so lousy tonight, she didn't argue when he pointed to the stands and told her to 'go sit.' It turned out that it was a good thing she was sitting down, and among friends. It was Rob's turn to compete and Jenny was trying to watch closely. Then, it happened again. Her vision began to fade, sounds intensified and she felt dizzy. This time, she didn't panic as she did the first time it had happened in Dr. Derkin's operating room. For one thing, she was already sitting down and she was among friends. Most of all, Rob was close by. She tried to keep her voice calm and reassuring as she told Julie, a longtime friend and wife of one of the competitors, what was happening.

Julie was the one who began to panic. "I'm going to get Rob!" Of course, were the first words that came out of her mouth.

"NO!" Jenny almost shouted. She did not want Rob to know. "There is nothing HE can do, just let him finish the contest. If you would just get me some water, I just need to sit here. This will pass in a few minutes. It has happened before." Jenny assured Julie. "I wouldn't have told you except I'm not sure I won't pass out or something. Just please, don't tell Rob."

"Are you sure?" Julie asked.

"Yes, I just need something to drink and I'll be fine."

Julie handed Jenny a bottle of water. "You look pale Jen. Can you see anything yet?"

"Some, I see shadows and light. It may take a little while, but I'll be good as new, promise."

Every few seconds Julie asked Jen if she could see yet. Jenny hated worrying her friend this way and it did seem that this time, her vision didn't return as quickly or fully as the last time.

Later, back in the horse barns they celebrated Rob's victory. Jenny did not want to tell him what had happened. They were going to have a barn dance in a little while and she just wanted to have some fun. But when she saw Julie giving her the eye, she knew if she didn't tell him, Julie would. Julie had agreed not to tell Rob until after the competition was over. But she made it clear to Jenny that if she didn't tell him after wards that he would be told, by her.

Jenny couldn't hide the migraine that was developing, why couldn't she just be like a normal and just have some joy in her life? Julie started walking towards them, facing the inevitable, she told Rob.

For the first time in a long time, Rob seemed genuinely worried about her. Maybe it was because so many of his friends and business associates were around. Or maybe, Jenny hoped, this weekend was the beginning of healing their wounded marriage.

Monday morning was the appointment with the ophthalmologist. He ordered a battery of tests. She was to have the first of many MRI's in two weeks; meanwhile she had an ocular angiogram, EEG, EKG, Pulmonary functions testing and several visual field tests. She felt like a test rat, indeed. A 'rash-rat.' But she wasn't alone. The other elven girls shared her feelings.

Mr. Stevens had warned them it was necessary to get full insight as to their medical problems 'post-exposure' before they could even begin to talk to CLS.

When the time came, CLS did not want to talk to them.

Chapter Eleven

Rob was in Florida at a horse show working as usual, it was sometimes hard to separate work from pleasure with him. He had some fairly wealthy clients and when they needed his help with their horses he was put up in the best hotels and paid quite well. He would still get to take along his own team of horses, but his priority became his client's horses. This time he was working for a construction firm in Wisconsin that sponsored a team of pulling horses. He was basically responsible for everything, shoeing, grooming and working them. It kept him very busy, yet they had time to play. He always ate at the best restaurants and went to the best bars and from time to time took in a country and western concert while 'working.'

Jenny hadn't wanted him to go this time. She had been through so much this past year with all of the tests and different changes in her health. She had been prescribed prednisone, a drug that had changed her body in so many ways. She cried a lot and was tired most of the time. She had gained so much weight, especially in her face! She hated the way she looked and obviously Rob did too. She had stopped praying months ago. She felt a gap widening not only between herself and Rob, but also between her and God. The only relationship that stayed the same was that between herself and her children and that was all that kept her sane. Even though they had both moved out of the house she was still so very close to them and kept in close contact. When Rob was away, she spent as much time as she could with her sons.

Jake was in his freshman year at the university, his apartment only about six blocks from the hospital. Jenny would often stop by his place and drop off donuts on her way to work in the mornings. He and Robbie both checked in with her often to make sure she was alright. She had raised them both in a Charismatic church. When they were just babies she had them dedicated to God. She knew they believed in the Lord, but somehow college and all of the classes on different cultures and religions can confuse young people. They began to question if Christ was really the only way to salvation. They had many serious talks about that very subject.

Jake couldn't understand why God had let his best friend die at the young age of sixteen, or why his Mom was now so sick. Even though Jenny tried to reassure him with the verse that Grandpa Jake had taught her so many years ago, he still questioned. "All things work together for the good...." Yeah, that was the verse. How could Jenny assure Jake that things really would work out for the best when she was having trouble believing it herself? How could she reinforce Jake's faith when she was having trouble with her own? She just hoped that God would keep his promise that if you 'bring up a child in the way they should go, they will not depart from it.' She hoped that someday both her sons would come full circle with their faith in God. When they were young they would sit outside on the swing and sing songs of faith as they played. They even quoted scripture to each other. Someday, she knew in her heart, they would come back to that faith. She hoped she would too.

Robbie lived just as close to Jake, but in the other direction. She saw him mostly on Sunday afternoons when he came to diner. He had a full time job and a rock and roll band on the side. He, like Jake, had distanced himself from the Lord through is late teens and early twenties. Robbie often had to be the man of the house when Rob wasn't home, helping Jenny with the horses. He still enjoyed them, a little. Jake, disliked them a lot!

Neither of her sons were what you would call 'mommy's boys' but they were certainly very close to Jenny and she was proud of that. When they were growing up she would always have honest heart to heart talks with them. There really wasn't anything they couldn't discuss as she never got angry with them or embarrassed by any subject they tossed at her. They were her friends as well as her sons, and she loved their relationship. She was so blessed by her children and so proud of them. They were in essence, her proof of God.

The boys didn't seem to have trouble being around her now like Rob did. It hurt them to see her health deteriorating, but they wanted to do what they could to help her get stronger. They watched her struggle with minor tasks, and when they went to eat she almost always ordered a sandwich to avoid running the risk of dropping her fork. Sewing had become a thing of the past and she was little help to Rob in the barn with the chores.

Rob saw the sleepless nights due to back pain, joint pain, headaches. She cried often and a lot. Many nights she would get out of bed and he would find her sitting on the sofa crying. She had grown short tempered. In the

103

twenty plus years of their marriage he had never seen her lose her temper or be sharp tongued with him like she was now. She has a short fuse with everyone these days. She was changing, and so were his feelings for her. Rob didn't deal well with sick people. He began to stay away from home more and more often.

Jenny had called him in Florida three times already that day. The first was just before noon.

"Hi Rob, how's the weather in Florida?" She casually asked.

"Raining, but it comes and goes, is it raining there?"

"No. It is just our normal gloomy February weather, cold and snowing."

"What do you want Jenny?" He asked his usual question to her when she called him when he was away from home.

"I want to ask you something."

"Is it important?"

"Yes, it is. How do you feel about having our case filed in federal court?" It was 'their' case as Mr. Stephens had filed on behalf of Rob too.

"I suppose that would be a good sign, it would show at least that things are progressing. Has it been filed?" He asked.

"Yes, this morning."

"Is that all you wanted?"

"Yes, I just wanted to talk to you and let you know it had been filed."

"If that's all you need, I was just on my way out to the barns to take care of the horses. I'll be there all day."

"I guess so."

"Ok, bye."

"Rob?" Jenny wanted to talk to him just a little longer, she missed him and he had been gone nearly two weeks this time.

"What is it Jen?" This time there was frustration in his voice.

"Nothing. Goodbye." Tears fell on her cheeks as she hung the receiver up.

Later in the day Mr. Stevens called to warn Jenny that since the case had been filed in Federal Court at the state building it could get some media attention. He wanted to warn her that reporters could be calling and tell her not to talk to them if they did. He had her rather nervous about the whole thing. Her first instinct was to call Rob again. She knew he would probably get upset with her so she waited. At least she tried to, a few hours later she did call him. He was her husband darn it and she needed him!

"Rob, I'm sorry to bother you again, but I needed to talk to you a minute."

"What NOW Jenny?" He was definitely irritated with her.

"Mr. Stevens called. He wanted to warn me, well, US, that there may be reporters calling us."

"Get real Jenny, why would reporters be calling us?"

"Because we filed a lawsuit in a Federal Court in our state capital is why!" Jenny was getting frustrated. Rob acted like it was killing him to take a minute to talk to her.

"People file cases in Federal Court everyday Jen. No reporters will call you."

"But Stevens thinks that because of all the controversy going on in the capital right now over that automotive deal, there may be even more reporters snooping around through public records than usual." Jenny said. "And Rob, he thinks they may try to reach you too."

"Again, I am in Florida Jen. They aren't going to try to reach me, and even if they did I am smart enough not to talk to them."

"You could be half way around the world for all they care Rob, if they think they have a story, they will find you."

"You are being irrational. Are the boys around?" He asked.

"No, it's Friday night. If you were young and single would you be sitting at home with your MOM?"

"Well I can't come home to hold your hand Jen! You will just have to get it together and try to get some sleep."

Jenny could hear the aggravation in his voice. This man who had once loved her so much, now only wanted to stay as far away from her as he possibly could, and talk to her as little as necessary.

"Father," Jen prayed to herself. "Why doesn't he understand how much I need him?"

"Alright, goodnight Rob." She had forgotten about the horse show being that night until that moment. " Rob, good luck tonight."

"Thanks, I probably won't call you when I get back to the hotel tonight, it will be late." Rob said. "And YOU need to rest. I'll call you tomorrow."

"Ok. Goodnight."

"Night." He said as he hung up the phone.

It was way past midnight when Rob got back to the phone. He thought about calling Jen to tell her he had gotten second place. It wasn't that he didn't still love her, he just wasn't 'in love' with her anymore. He still worried about her. He just didn't know how to deal with this new person she had become. And he didn't want to. So he lay down on the bed and began to drift off to sleep, then the phone rang. He picked up the receiver but all he could hear was sobbing.

"Jen, is that you?   I can't understand a word you are saying, what's wrong?"   He hoped nothing had happened to the boys. She called him a lot crying anymore. He never knew when there was something serious or just her mood.

"Jen, you have to stop crying and tell me what is going on."

She tried to compose herself by blowing her nose and taking a deep breath.

"Rob," she sniffed. "The phone hasn't stopped ringing all evening. Reporters are calling from different newspapers all across the country. Not just local Rob, everywhere!" She blew her nose again.

"Why?"

"The Associated Press picked up our story. Rob, I keep telling them that I have 'no comment' just like Stevens said to do. But they start yelling and asking questions and threatening to come to our house if I don't talk to them." She sniffed again. "Rob, I need you."

Rob was worried, she sounded hysterical. And what good could he do, he was in Florida and she was in Michigan.

"Jen, do you still have those pills the doc gave you to help you sleep?" Normally he didn't like for her to take those pills, they made her so groggy and disconnected. Tonight, they seemed to be exactly what she needed.

"Yes, but you know I hate taking them, especially when I am here alone."

"I know, but I think you should tonight." He said. "Listen to me Jen, when we hang up, I want you to first, turn the answering machine on in the living room. Are you listening Jen?"

"Yes, I'm listening."

"After you do that, take one of those pills and then unplug the phone in the bedroom and go lay down." Rob's voice was stern, he sounded like he was talking to one of the kids when they were small. "Jen, understand what I am saying to you? Will you do that for me?"

"Yes, I will Rob. I didn't even thing about unplugging the phone in the bedroom."

"Of course you didn't, you aren't thinking at all right now, you are too upset." He said. "Jen, I'm sorry I'm not there tonight, really." He meant it.

"I know Rob, me too."

"Now, please do as I told you."

"Yes Boss," she managed a giggle. "I will."

"Goodnight, I'll call you in the morning." Rob said.

"Night, Rob." She said as he hung up the phone. She wanted so badly to hear him say 'I love you.' But Rob seldom spoke those words to her anymore. Only when she would ask him, and even then he would just say that she should know that he did and he shouldn't have to tell her. But she didn't know that anymore, she needed to hear it. But Rob, could no longer say it.

Before Rob returned home, the news media had their story. It was all over the papers as they expected it would be. The associated press carried the story coast to coast with the headlines reading: "MICHIGAN HEALTH CARE WORKERS SUE TWO MAJOR MEDICAL SUPPLY COMPANIES OVER DEFECTIVE SURGICAL GOWNS." Or, "CHEMICALS LEFT IN SURGICAL GOWNS CAUSED LASTING ILLNESS FOR SEVERAL SURGICAL NURSES."

Neither Jenny nor Rob had really wanted to file this lawsuit. They would have settled out of court. CLS wouldn't hear of it. The girls all had serious health problems. Some were getting worse by the day. Someone was responsible and someone needed to help with their medical expenses.

Everyone knew that lawsuits took time, but how much time was the major question. Once the word was out that the case had been actually filed in Federal Court, things got even worse at work. Newspaper clippings showed up on bulletin boards in the nurse's lounge, on the doors of the operating rooms they worked in, on their lockers. Everyone was questioning them.

"So, Jen, how much money are you suing for? Millions?"

"What are you going to do with all your money?"

"Way to go Jen! You can retire and live a life of luxury, we're friends aren't we?"

One comment after another was tossed at them. Not just to Jenny, but to all of the 'rash-rats.' Remarks came from surgeons, anesthesiologists, private assistants and other staff members.

Jenny tried to ignore their comments and chalk them up to ignorance. It was hard. She would gladly give any amount of money just to have her health back, and Rob. How could people be so hateful? Some of them were genuinely concerned, the ones she worked the closest with. They were the ones who saw firsthand how this had all taken a toll on her.

Because of her sensitivity to light, Jenny now had to wear sunglasses inside the operating room. She had to shield her eyes from the bright fluorescent lighting. This led to her being called; "Rob-scrub" or "Hollywood." She needed to use eye drops several times a day to keep the moisture in her eyes. She started dropping things a lot and often had trouble opening sterile supplies. She couldn't hold a retractor very long without losing her grip on it. She began to forget the names of instruments and would back away from the operating table whenever she became dizzy. Her eyes had dark circles under them from the stress and exhaustion.

111

Migraine headaches, dizzy spells, fatigue and recurrent bladder infections caused her to begin to miss a lot of work. She had never been sick before this. She had missed so much work lately that she was determined to go on to work even though when she woke up this morning, her right arm was completely numb and tingling.

Later that morning, while scrubbed in on a case, not only was it numb and tingling. She could not move her arm at all. With the peripheral neuropathy that she had developed it wasn't at all uncommon for her to have difficulty moving her arm when it went numb. So far it hadn't happened at work, until now. It had never felt quite so 'heavy' before either. Jenny actually had to pick her right arm up and move it with her left. The tingling and numbness then began to extend down her whole right side and she began to feel that heavy sensation extending into her right leg as well. For the second time, she had to be led out of the operating room and taken to the lounge to lie down.

Lisa came into the lounge as soon as she heard about Jenny.

"What's going on Dale?" She teased her. "We're a team you know, remember me? Chip?"

"I wish I knew." Jenny replied. "I still have no feeling on my right side and I can't move it at all."

"Did you call anyone?"

"Not yet, I can't dial the phone." Jenny replied trying to lighten the mood.

"Smart ass!" Lisa was worried. "Do you want me to call Rob for you?"

"No, he isn't there anyway, gone again." Seemed he was always gone these days.

"What about the boys?"

"Robbie is in Lansing, visiting a friend. Jake should be out of classes though. I was kind of waiting on him to be out of his last class before I tried to reach him."

"I'll call him for you." Lisa told her.

"Ok.

"Ah, were they trying to reach some one for you or did they just dump you in the nurse's lounge and forget about you?" Lisa had about had it with all the snippy remarks and the way a lot of people were treating them.

"Barbara was going to try to reach Dr. Harris at the University for me. You might check to see if she reached her."

"Ok, I'll check on that and give Jake a call." She winked at Jenny as she left the room and yelled. "Stay here! Don't take off anywhere!"

"Right, like I'm going to run off with my favorite movie star to Hawaii or something."

"You would if you could!"

Barbara had reached Dr. Harris and had her on the line. She was transferring the call to Jenny in the lounge. Lisa handed Jen the phone and she held it with her left hand.

"Dr. Harris." She breathed a sigh of relief at the sound of her Neurologists voice. "It's Jenny Reed."

"They tell me you are numb and can't move very well Jenny, tell me what happened."

Jenny described the incident to Dr. Harris.

"Can you come to the University Emergency Room? I will be a few hours before I can get away to see you but my associate, Dr. Grayson will meet you there."

"It would be at least three hours before I can get there. Remember, YOU are a three hour drive away from me. And I'd rather see you anyway. But if you aren't free then I will have to see Dr. Grayson.

"DRIVE?" Dr. Harris protested. "You can't drive anywhere being completely numb on one side!"

"Thanks for the advice, but I sort of had that figured out all ready. I will get someone to bring me."

"Ok, see you in the Emergency room in a few hours."

Lisa had reached Jake at work. He had gone straight from class to his job.

"Jake, it's Lisa, your Mom needs you to come and pick her up at the hospital. Can you do that?"

"What's wrong with Mom? Is she OK? Is she sick?"

"She is ok Jake; she just can't drive herself home." Lisa didn't feel it was her place to tell Jake that Jenny needed him to drive her to the University ER, at least not over the phone.

"Sure, I'll be right there. Where should I pick her up?"

"Beside the elevators in the parking garage, you know the one?"

"Yeah, sure. Be there in five minutes." Jake told her.

Jenny still couldn't walk to Lisa had to use a wheelchair to take her outside. Lisa stayed with her until Jake got there. She watched as his car rounded the corner and she saw the fear in the young man's face when he saw his Mom in a wheelchair. He quickly bounded out of the car towards them.

"Mom, are you ok? What happened? Why are you in this wheelchair?" He couldn't stop asking questions long enough for either of them to squeeze in an answer.

Finally, Lisa interrupted him. "She is going to be fine Jake, but she really needs your help right now."

"I'm ok Jake, thanks for coming to get me. I'm sort of having a little trouble with my right side. My arm and leg went numb. You may have to take me to University Medical Center if your Dad isn't home by the time we get there." Jenny told him.

Jake helped his Mom into his car then politely thanked Lisa for staying with her until he arrived. He promised to call her that evening to let her know how Jenny was. For a nineteen year old, Jake was a mature young man.

All the way home Jenny was inwardly praying and talking to God. "Remember Lord, all things should turn out good, for those that love you. I love you! I don't understand you right now, but I love you. Why is this happening to me?"

Rob was still not home when they got there. Jake said he would take her on to University Medical Center. (UMC) Jenny thought she should at least give Rob a call and tell him where they were going in case he got back home before they did. She reached him on his cell phone.

"Hi Rob. I sort of have a little problem. I can't feel my right side and it doesn't want to move much. Jake is driving me to UMC. Dr. Harris wanted me to come right away." She rushed the words out, hating to even call Rob. "Where are you?"

"I'm already over half way home. I should only be about another thirty minutes. Tell Jake to stay with you till I get home, I will take you."

116

"I'm supposed to meet Dr. Harris when I get there. I told her it would be a couple of hours. Are you sure you don't want Jake to go ahead and drive me, he doesn't mind."

"Jenny, I said: I WILL TAKE YOU." He was adamant. "Just tell Jake to stay with you until I get there."

"Ok, be careful." She didn't need him getting into a wreck hurrying home because of her. "I'm not in any pain, just numb and tingling."

"See you in a few minutes." Rob said and hung up.

And a few minutes it was. He was home in less than a half an hour, so much for driving carefully.

Jake had wanted to go with them to UMC but Rob assured him that he could take care of his Mom for him and that he should go back to work.

By the time they had arrived at UMC, Jenny thought she was feeling much better. She was still numb and it was still difficult to move her right side, but not impossible. Dr. Harris came in to examine her.

After looking into her pupils and asking her tons of questions she pulled out a safety pin and began to touch Jenny's arm with it.

"Sharp or dull?" She asked.

"Dull, I guess. I can't really feel it." Jenny replied.

"Can you move your leg?"

"Yes, it just feels like it weighs a ton and I have to really focus to make it move."

By this time Jenny could feel pressure, but not pain and she could move it very slowly. Dr. Harris wanted to keep Jenny overnight in the hospital. Jenny refused to stay. After much debate, Jenny held her ground. She was going back home with Rob and no one was changing her mind. Dr. Harris scheduled some tests that would be done in a few days at UMC and Jenny would have to make the trip back down for them. But she didn't care. She wasn't staying in the hospital.

Within the next week, Jenny had two more MRI's and several more ocular exams and she looked like she had been attacked by a fleet of vampire bats there were so many puncture wounds on her body. She had an appointment with Dr. Harris late in the afternoon for test results.

"Jenny, I think it is time you consider going on medical leave."

"NO way! I need to work, I LOVE my job!" Jenny protested.

"You have peripheral neuropathy Jenny. These spells are not going to stop. I just hope they don't get worse. There is no evidence that they will, but there is no evidence that they won't either." Dr. Harris told her.

"Not yet, please, I want to work a little longer." Jenny pleaded with her doctor.

"I can't force you to stop working Jenny, I'm just telling you that it is my medical opinion that you should no longer be working. Think about it. If not for yourself, consider it for your patient's safety."

"I will." Jenny said, but in reality, she wasn't even giving it a second thought!

Jenny was glad she had made the trip to UMC today by herself. On the way home she stopped at a roadside park and sat and cried.

"Why Father? Why have you allowed this to happen? I thought you loved me, I thought I was your daughter and I was protected! I thought you wanted me to work in this field, and why is my marriage falling apart?! Don't you still love me? Have I done something wrong? Is this how you love your children?" Jenny was angry at God.

Jenny sobbed into the steering wheel of the car for over twenty minutes. What would she do if she couldn't work? What good would she be? Just a few short years ago she was a wife and mother, she had a family. Now, Rob was staying away from home for longer and longer periods of times. She was lucky if he was home seven days out of a whole month! Both Robbie and Jake had moved out of the home the same summer, in 1990. Robbie turned twenty-one that July and had moved into his own place. Jake went away to college just two weeks later. Talk about empty nest syndrome! If it hadn't been for her dog, Jenny would have gone bonkers! Now, it seems as if God had 'moved out' on her too.

119

She had never felt so alone in her life. But things were just beginning.

Chapter Twelve

By November of 1992, Jenny was really struggling to stay at work. She changed her schedule, both she and Lisa had jumped at the opportunity to work the twelve hour shifts when they were offered. Now she and Lisa worked only five days out of fourteen, but they were twelve hour days. It was nice because she was able to have a series of days in a row off, maybe if she was lucky she would only be sick on her days off.

Jenny's memory was really starting to deteriorate. One day she drove into town to buy some milk at the nearest pantry, just a two-mile driver from her home. One-mile east and one-mile west and presto, you are at the pantry. No biggie, that is until she got into the car to go home. Suddenly, she could not remember how to get 'home'. The most horrifying feeling swept over her as she knew that home was close by, she could even picture the farm in her mind. Yet, she couldn't remember how to get there. She thought to herself how ridiculous this seemed as she had lived on that farm for twenty years! She sat in the parking lot of the pantry with her car running as she tried to imagine which way to go when she turned onto the highway. She felt like she had just entered the twilight zone! Finally, she began to just drive. Right or left? Her instinct told her left. About a quarter of a mile later it was if the blind had been lifted on a dark room and let the sun in. She remembered where she was and how to continue to home. She felt so dumb, yet so frightened. She really had not been able for a few moments, how to find her way back home and she was just two miles from home!

Once inside her house, Jenny called Mr. Stevens and told him what had just happened. A few weeks later he called her back.

"Jenny, I want you and a few of the other girls to see a new doctor I have found."

"Come on Mr. Stevens! We already see twenty different doctors now!" She wasn't exaggerating! "Who is he and why do we need to see him?"

"Have you ever heard of Dr. Sanders?"

"No. Why? Should I have?"

"He is a world renowned specialist in the field of neurology."

"Where and when?" Jenny asked. She hated the idea of seeing more doctors.

"New York City, end of the week. You and Lisa will go first, then in a couple of weeks two more of you will go."

"WHAT? Are you kidding? NEW YORK?" Jenny said. "At the end of *this* week? We need time to arrange our days off!"

"It's already been arranged Jenny. I talked to Barb this morning. You and Lisa leave Thursday morning."

"What's wrong with Dr. Harris? She is the Neurologist you have us seeing now."

"Jenny, we have a multi-million dollar lawsuit going on here, we need world renowned doctors backing us up. You don't go up against big guns with water pistols." He was getting irritated. "Now, are you going to do as I say, or not?"

"Do I have a choice?" She asked.

"No."

Jenny and Lisa traveled together many times. Jenny was on the Board of Directors for the Association of Surgical Technologists and Lisa would always go to conference with her whenever the hospital allowed. They had been to Pittsburg, Boston, Las Vegas, Chicago, Indianapolis, Denver and Minneapolis for national conferences as well as many local and regional meetings. No matter where they went they had fun. Lisa always over packed. Fashionista that she was, she not only had to match her shoes and purses to her outfit, but her sunglasses too! Their adventures were always amazing. One time they rode in an elevator with many of the players from the Houston Rockets basketball team during the championship finals in Boston! In Pittsburg they rode in an elevator with Bob Segar. In Chicago they were in a sports bar eating with half the members of the American League baseball team! Once in Vegas, they literally almost tripped over Wayne Newton in a corridor. Wherever they went, they had an adventure. The two of them always enjoyed traveling together. But this was one trip that neither of them looked forward to.

"Remember Lisa, this is just an OVERNIGHT trip. You only need one bag with your pajamas and one change of clothes!"

"She'll never make it!" Jim, Lisa's husband laughed. "Not my wife."

"Ok you two. I know when I'm being harassed." Lisa yelled from her bedroom. "I can pack just one bag if I want to, I think."

They went to work as usual that Thursday morning but they took their overnight bags with them in the trunk of Jenny's car. Mr. Stevens had arranged for them to leave work early enough to catch their flight to New York. This was no pleasure trip, no time for sightseeing. However they did see the Statue of Liberty and the New York Mets stadium from the air as they landed at LaGuardia International Airport. It was nearly seven-thirty p.m. when they arrived at the hotel.

"Look Jen!" Lisa exclaimed as she gazed out of the window of the hotel's fourteenth floor. "NEW YORK city! Right outside of our window! Let's go out for super and look around."

"Lisa, we are in the middle of the Bronx. If you want to go out, go for it. I'm staying right here and ordering room service." Country girl that she was she had no desire to go roaming around New York City, especially not in the dark, in the Bronx. The only big city she had been to that she really liked was Denver and she had to

124

admit if it had been Denver outside her window instead of New York, wild horses couldn't keep her inside.

"I'm too tired to go out anyway." Lisa admitted. "What sounds good from room service?"

"Anything expensive! I didn't want to take this trip and since they law firm made us, and are footing the bill, it is all on them." Jenny said. "Let's order. We need to get some sleep, our day starts early tomorrow. We have to be at the Einstein Institute before 7am."

"That's right, and we have to check out of the hotel before we leave since our flight is at 5:30 p.m. tomorrow afternoon. We have no time to see the city anyway."

"That's too bad." Jenny said, not one bit sincere. "See, aren't you glad you only packed one bag? It will be hard enough tote one bag around all day much less a luggage rack full!"

"Sure am! Guess you were right for once." Lisa laughed.

"Whoa! Did I hear right? You admitted you were wrong and I was right?"

"Shut up and call room service!" Lisa smiled.

Their schedule was even more rigorous the next day than they had imagined. Together they were introduced to Dr. Sanders and two of his staff members, Dr. Glass and Dr. Bennett. They were taken in different directions, passing only in the hall as they occasionally switched rooms and doctors.

At lunchtime Dr. Bennett ordered food for all of them at the local deli. They let them take a small break, long enough to eat. Lisa and Jenny were taken to one of the office so they could eat together. They compared notes on how the morning was going. The doctors had their lunch in one of the conference rooms, obviously doing the same thing.

"Did you do that ink blot thing?" Lisa asked Jenny.

"Yes, the memory game too." Jenny said. "I don't think I passed that one. Were you asked a thousand and ten questions too?"

"I guess so. Everyone is nice here but if one more person hugs me and says "God Bless you." I think I may scream!" Lisa said.

"I know, it feels like they know something I don't." Jenny said. "It's almost like they think we have one foot in the grave and the other on a banana peel."

They both got the impression that the news of their fate was better known to strangers than to themselves.

"You know, I have always heart that New Yorkers were rude and snobbish. That hasn't been the case. Everyone has been really nice to us." Jenny observed. "Even the cab drivers, I think. It's kind of hard to tell since they didn't speak English!"

"I know, it is the opposite of what I expected too." Lisa agreed. "However, I have been wondering when they are going to bring out the big cage and the giant wheel to put us in to see how fast we can make it turn."

Dr. Glass stuck his head in the door along with Dr. Bennett.

"Break time is over girls, back to work. We have a lot more tests to get done today." Dr. Bennett said. "We have to split you up this afternoon to get done in time. But we promise to get you back together in time for your flight home."

"Jenny," Dr. Bennett directed his attention to her. "I've called a cab for you. Here is the address to give to the cab driver." He said, as he handed her a slip of paper with an address on it and some cash for the cab driver. "Don't worry, we won't lose you! Where you are going is just across campus." He then handed her yet another slip of paper. "This is the name of the clinic you are to go to. Just show them this at the information desk, they are expecting you. Then have them call me when you are finished and I will personally pick you up. Okay?"

"I guess, but I don't like the idea of getting in a cab in this city alone." She said. "If he drops me at the wrong place I may never find you guys again! I got lost in my own hometown a few weeks ago."

"You will be fine, I promise." Dr. Bennett laughed. "Now go, your cab is waiting."

127

This was yet another eye exam. She had to try to focus on the black and white checks on the screen that was constantly moving. The red dot was where her eyes were supposed to hold focus. She could not keep her eyes focused at all. Her head began to spin and she felt one of her more intense migraines coming on. She felt the pressure behind her eyes building, yes, definitely getting a migraine. Just what she needed! If she didn't take the pills Dr. Harris had prescribed for her she wouldn't be able to think clearly because of her headache. If she took the pills, she wouldn't be able to think clearly because she would be drugged! But the eye testing was done. Even if they didn't say so, she did. She couldn't go through another test.

Dr. Bennett came to pick her up in front of the building as he had promised. He was taking her to yet another clinic where she would meet up with Lisa. It was getting late in the afternoon and almost time to head to the airport.

Lisa was being tested directly behind the screen where Jenny was sitting. It was reassuring to hear her voice.

"Are we done yet?" Lisa asked.

"Yes, but I still have to run this test on Jenny." A voice answered. "I think she is waiting for us now."

"Will it take as long as it did for me?"

"I expect it will."

"We have a plane to catch at 5:30." Lisa said.

"When?" The voice asked.

"Our flight leaves at 5:30 p.m." Lisa answered.

"In that case, we are done. I'll call you a cab. It takes at least an hour to get to the airport from here at this time of day."

Jenny looked at her watch. It was already 4:00 p.m. This was one time she was really looking forward to getting on a plane. Jenny and Lisa were too tired to talk much; usually no one could get a word in edgewise around them. Not on this flight, they didn't talk at all, they just slept.

Chapter Thirteen

Mr. Stevens called a meeting with his twelve clients. He met them at the hospital in the conference room. Administration was still 'outwardly' cooperating with them, while 'inwardly' giving them a very difficult time. Mr. Stevens had agreed that his clients wouldn't name them in the lawsuit if they cooperated.

"Good afternoon ladies." He said as he began the meeting. "The reason I called this meeting with you is that I have something important to tell you."

They were all on the edge of their chairs hoping he was going to say that CLS had agreed to settle out of court.

Instead he told them, "Depositions are going to begin soon. I will be with each of you while you are being deposed. We will also have a court stenographer in the room besides the two opposing attorneys."

"We heard they had already been here talking to and deposing the hospital administration this week." Jamie said. "Will ours be done here also?"

"No, your will be done at my firm, in a conference room there."

"Will we be given the day off from work to go, or will we have to take vacation days or call in sick?" Melissa asked.

"I have already cleared it with your supervisors for each of you to have the necessary days off work." He answered.

"How soon do we start these depositions?" Jenny asked.

"Next month. Yours is first Jenny, and it will take at least two days."

"TWO days? Just for them to ask me questions? Why?"

"Yes two days, you are one of the most severely affected of the group. Trust me; it is to your benefit that you are going first."

The news that she was going to be the first to be questioned was unsettling but as the time grew closer Jenny was beginning to feel a sense of relief. At least hers would be over first, and it was a positive sign for their case that depositions were beginning.

She arrived at the offices of Newman and Chapel around 7:30 am. Mr. Stevens had instructed her to arrive at least a half an hour before they began to go over some documents with her and put her at ease. He gave her a complete tour of their legal offices. It was the first time she or any of the girls had been to his office. It was very impressive. There were over one hundred attorneys in the firm. The building was nothing less than a skyscraper in comparison to the surrounding ones and it stood directly across from the capitol building. Jenny hoped his legal antics were as impressive as his office.

"This is very nice Mr. Stevens." She told him.

"Jenny, we have been at this case for some time now, don't you think it's time you called me Wayne?" He really wanted her to relax.

"I suppose." She said. "This is very nice, Wayne."

Back in the conference room he offered her a cup of coffee. She was far too nervous for more coffee so she opted for water. A few minutes later a tall, willowy blonde entered the room. Wayne introduced her to Jenny as Ms. Chapman, Attorney at Law, representing CLS. Jenny stood and shook her hand. Ms. Chapman projected a very stern and professional image. Hard to pull off when you have Barbie doll good looks. She was young, beautiful and intelligent. Her intent was clearly to intimidate Jenny. Normally, she could have done just that based on her beauty alone. But as nervous as Jenny was, she wasn't about to let anyone intimidate her, Barbie doll perfect or not.

Jenny knew she had the truth on her side and while she hadn't been attending church on a regular basis, she still believed in her Lord. She had distanced herself from Him a little and had even grown angry as she had been blaming God for her marriage, her health, to be truthful, Jenny was angry with everyone and everything right now. But she still believed in God and while it seemed hard to do, she did trust Him still. She could still hear Grandpa Jake's words as he spoke to her in that burned out church so long ago. "Remember Jenny, if you love Jesus, even in the worst times of your life, something good will happen."

This was definitely the worst time of her life, so far. And she still loved the Lord, so somehow she knew she would get through this with His help.

Ms. Chapman questioned her non-stop for the next three hours. She wanted to know everything about Jenny from the birthmark on her side to the shampoo she used on her hair.

Sitting in the straight upright position that the chair forced her into had caused Jenny's neck and back to ache. Not to mention the things the fluorescent lights were doing to her eyes. When they moved for a lunch break, the first thing Jenny wanted was an Anaprox tablet for the pain down her spine and in her head. Her purse was in the chair directly behind Ms. Chapman.

"Excuse me." Jenny said as she reached behind Ms. Chapman for her purse. She placed it on the table and quickly reached for her prescription bottle. Ms. Chapman watched her every move.

"Oh, I'm so sorry." She said with mock sympathy. "Did I give you a headache?" She smiled.

"No, you didn't, the lights have." Jenny responded.

She leaned forward onto the table with crossed arms and an arched back.

"Honey, all you have to do is cry 'uncle'. Ms. Chapman hissed at Jenny in a tone that could have landed her a part in the next Disney flick as an evil serpent or witch!

The fire must have sparked in Jenny's eyes. She stood up and leaned across the table in Ms. Chapman's direction about to give her a piece of her mind when Wayne grabbed Jenny's arm and pulled her back.

"And all your client has to do is admit their guilt, MS. CHAPMAN." Wayne said as he spun Jenny toward him.

"Come on Jenny, you need a break." He led her to the door.

All through lunch Wayne assured her that she was doing just fine. Her answers were precise and to the point just as he had instructed her. He warned her that Ms. Chapman would probably come on even stronger after lunch, telling Jenny she couldn't let the woman get to her. Jenny was expecting that, and she was ready.

Jenny sat through another four hours of intense and often very personal questions. She asked questions about her marriage, Rob's business and how Rob's infidelity in the past had affected her. She was very intrusive and rude even going so far as to question Jenny about her sex life. Jenny felt the questions should have been limited to the chemical exposure and her health since and that her sex life was none of their business. At one point Jenny had to ask to be excused. She then went to the ladies room where she prayed.

"Lord, I know I am supposed to control my tongue and that your word says: Behold how great a forest is set aflame by such a small fire. I think it is in the book of James. Help me to control my tongue. I want so much to give Ms. Chapman a piece of my mind. Help me, to remain calm." Back in the conference room with Ms. Chapman interrogating her, it almost felt as if Jenny had a guardian angel sitting on her shoulder whispering to her. "Stay calm Jenny, you can do it, guard your words." Were it not for the presence of that wee small voice, Jenny may have told the attorney to stick to the subject at hand and keep her nose out of her personal life. When she returned home from the deposition that night she was exhausted, and she had one more day to go. She expected another day of the same torment. However her second day wasn't quite as bad. Ms. Chapman did seem to focus on the matter of business. The day went quickly and they finished around noon, relief flooded Jenny. Her interrogation was over.

Chapter Fourteen

"I can't believe you are on call again tonight Jenny!" Rob said as he watched her gather up her clothes into a neat little pile with her shoes and car keys on the top of them.

"Yes, but it is just back up call." Jenny replied. "I shouldn't be called in unless it is something really drastic."

Rob hated it when she was on call. It would mean that the moment the phone rang she would jump up and leave the house and he wouldn't know when she would be back. It interrupted her rest, and his.

The phone did ring, Jenny should have known. She had just drifted off to sleep. Most of the time it was hard for her to rest when she was on call but since it was 'back up call' she managed to fall asleep fairly early tonight.

"What is it tonight?" She asked the hospital operator as she slid her jeans on.

"Stabbing." The voice on the other end of the line responded. "The patient is on their way up to the operating room as we speak. They told me they would need the backup team as well."

"On my way." Jenny hung up the phone and dashed out of the door.

She arrived to find a twenty-year old boy fighting for his life on the surgery table. His chest was already opened by the time she got there and Dr. Spears was up to his elbows in the young man's blood. So much was happening at once. When Jenny walked into the room she was bombarded with questions. Dr. Spears and Dr. Vance were too busy to even notice that she had arrived, but her fellow staff members were delighted to see her. Everyone there tonight, with the exception of Jenny and the doctors, were new personnel, fresh off orientation, just as she had been so many years ago. Now, Jenny knew why they had called her.

Steve, the new scrub tech that worked afternoons was especially glad to see her. He literally had his instruments tossed into a big pile on his back table. Making it difficult if not impossible to find what he needed. Jenny knew how that felt; she had been in that situation more than once as the patient arrived in the operating room before the instruments did. You had to first sort out your knife handle, scissors and a few clamps and leave the rest in the instrument pans or tossed on the table. There was no time to arrange everything in the nice, neat orderly manner that you normally did.

Under controlled circumstances, everyone sat their back tables up much in the same order and sequence of instruments. This made it easier when you had to come in and relieve someone for a break or for lunch, or simply take over a case. If everyone's back table is sat up the same, it is an easy transition. But sometimes an orderly table just didn't happen, like tonight.

Jenny quickly took her place next to Dr. Spears; he was working alone and had no first assistant to help him. No wonder Steve's table looked like he had just dumped the pan onto it. He couldn't even try to straighten it up when he was acting as 'scrub tech' and 'first assistant' at the same time. He had to help Dr. Spears retract the tissue so he could see to find the bleeding.

Stepping up on the stool next to Dr. Spears, Jenny asked.

"What can I do to help you?"

"Jenny!" How long have you been here?" He asked.

"Just a couple of minutes, what have we got?"

"Knife wound, losing way too much blood way too fast." He answered. "I can't find where all this blood is coming from. Steve, give Jen a retractor."

Jenny was pulling with all her strength on the retractor, trying to lift the young man's rib cage enough that Dr. Spears could get a better view. Her grip was starting to slide and it was becoming so difficult to hold on to it. As she held the retractor she began to scan the room. She didn't see the Cardio-Vascular cabinets.

"Steve, do you have any Cardio instruments out?"

"Not yet, they are in the room though, just not opened." He said as he nodded his head towards his table. "As you can see, the patient arrived before the instruments. I only tossed out what we needed to crack his chest first. Does that tell you my situation?"

"Sure does."

She knew that Steve had only the very basic instrumentation out. There had been no time for anything else. The circulating nurse was busy helping the anesthesiologist hang blood. But now, getting the proper instruments had to be a priority. Once they found the bleeding, they would need the proper clamps to control it.

"Carol, get that Cardio-Vascular cabinet out of the hallway and into this room, NOW!" Jenny took control. "Kelly, open up that C-V tray and when the cabinet gets here throw Steve out some Cardio-Vascular sutures. He is going to need some vessel loops, hydra grips and rubber shods too."

"I better get the crash cart too." Carol said as she came back into the room with the CV cabinet.

"Good thinking Carol."

Jenny didn't mean to sound like a drill Sargent, but at this point, she didn't care. The patient was her priority.

"Glad you made it Jen." Dr. Spears said. "Everyone has been doing a great job, just good to have some experience in the room." He had his arm elbow deep in the young man's chest.

"Damn, I found the bleeding." He said, in a tone that told Jenny it wasn't good. "The knife went through is lung and punctured his pulmonary artery. CV CLAMP!" He shouted.

Steve thrust one into his hand as quickly as Jenny could have herself. He was doing a great job.

"I think we are too late Ken." Dr. Vance said. "I haven't had a pressure on him for several minutes. He didn't stand a chance with that kind of injury."

Despite everyone's best effort, the young man died. He would never grow to be an old man. He would never have children of his own.

As Jenny helped Steve and the others clean up the room that night, she realized how important quick thinking and quick response was to everyone that works in the operating room. The ability to think fast and act even faster was the difference between life and death. Jenny's ability to think fast had been diminishing along with her grip and sensitivity in her hands.

Just last week she couldn't remember how to stop her car while she was driving! She forgot where the brakes were! She went past the end of her driveway and between the two big trees in the back yard as she frantically tried to remember how to stop it. 'Oh, yeah, brakes...where are they?' She had thought to herself. Thank God there was nothing there to hit, no fence on their property line as she slammed on the brakes, sending the sacks of groceries to the floor.

What if she had been the first call team tonight? Would has have been able to respond fast enough? In her heart, she knew the answer, although she didn't want to face it. Doing her job was becoming more and more difficult with each passing day. Just two years ago she was among the best, most confident scrubs in the department. After the exposure to the chemicals, all that changed. She was now beginning to forget the names of some of the instruments, forgetting what different surgeons used for sutures and other little idiosyncrasies each of them had. These were the things she should have known, things she use to know because she had worked with these surgeons for over twelve years. Sometimes her grip made it impossible to hold onto a retractor for any length of time, she even had problems opening sterile supplies. Her vision was becoming and equal problem. Even though she was wearing tinted lenses, the bright lights were still reflecting on the metal instruments to the point of nearly blinding her vision. She really struggled to do Laparoscopic Gallbladders' or Corneal Implants where the room lights were off and you did the procedure by watching a monitor.

While everyone knew how difficult those cases were for her now, they seemed to be the ones she was regularly assigned to. Adding to her problems was the recurring contact dermatitis that forced her to be restricted from scrubbing at times for a week or more.

Jenny continued to be bombarded with thoughts as she left the operating room. She sat on the bench in the woman's dressing room with her head in her hands, thinking, wondering what she should do.

Just last week her supervisor suggested that she consider transferring out of the surgical department. They thought she might be more 'useful' in Central Supply, where the 'gas ethylene oxide sterilizers were.

When she had told Dr. Harris where the department supervisor planned to transfer her, Dr. Harris was appalled!

"THAT is INSANE!" She was furious when Jenny told her. "What are they trying to do? Drive the nails in your coffin? You have absolutely NO business anywhere NEAR an ethylene oxide sterilizer!"

"But what if I really can't continue to scrub?" Jenny had asked her.

"Be honest with yourself Jenny." She tried to sound reassuring. "The recurring contact dermatitis is one of the more minor of your problems. Peripheral Neuropathy, visual problems, headaches and memory are what is affecting your job the most. And those things would be a problem to you no matter what job you were doing."

"What are you saying?" Jenny asked.

"Only what I have been trying to tell you for several months now." She replied. "You need to stop working for a while."

"You mean, go on workman's comp? I don't want to do that!"

"Jenny, when you stick yourself with a needle, do you feel it?"

"No." Jenny said.

"I know that is a danger to you, you could contact aides, or hepatitis from the patients."

"I don't want to give up my job!"

"Jenny, I understand that. But if you won't protect yourself, think of your patients." Dr. Harris had been sincere. "You are not only endangering your life, but your patients as well. You know that don't you Jen?" She had reached for Jenny's hand. "Jenny, you do know that don't you?"

"Yes, Yes, I know that." Jenny burst into tears.

"Then let me take you off work for a little while. Who knows, maybe a little rest and you could return to work in a few months."

"May I have some time to think about it?"

"Just call me when you are ready."

On the way home that night, after losing the young man on the operating table, Jenny kept thinking of all the 'what if's'. What if she had been on first call, what if she hadn't been able to think clearly enough to respond to the needs of the team that night? What if she had lost her grip on the retractor?

The next day, Jenny was opening sterile supplies for her case and dropped a glass medicine cup on the floor. It shattered sending shards of glass all over the room. Dr. Harris's voice echoed loud and clear in her mind. "You are not only endangering yourself, but your patients as well." The last thing Jenny every wanted was to be a danger to her patients. She was in this profession to help people, not harm them. She began to pray for strength, strength to do what she knew she must.

She walked out of the operating room and called Dr. Harris. "Will you fax an off work slip to the hospital and take me off work for now?" She asked.

"Of course Jenny, effective when?" Dr. Harris had been expecting this call.

"Immediately." Jen answered.

"What happened?" Dr. Harris asked.

"I just realized you were right."

It was May 7th 1993.

Chapter Fifteen

The summer months were not that difficult to get through. Now Jenny had the time to do some of the things she had wanted to do before. She planted a rose garden. She had always loved her father's roses but never had her own. On Mother's Day, Robbie bought her a beautiful scarlet tea rose. It became the center of her garden. Soon it was joined by seventeen other varieties and colors of roses. Tending her flowers was something she was still able to do. She didn't need to think fast or respond quickly, no precise movement necessary, except of course to dodge the occasional bumblebee.

Joining her rose garden was an herb garden, this she really enjoyed. She had started making her own potpourri, bath oil and specialty teas. She made 'sleep pillows' out of different herbs used for relaxation such as Lavender and Passionflower. She just had to limit her time in the sun. Most of the time when she was outside, she wore a big floppy hat and had on long sleeves and sunglasses. It made her feel like an old woman.

Rob bought her a riding lawnmower so she could take care of the yard. She needed something to be responsible for, it didn't matter what it was. Besides, she loved mowing the yard even with the old push mower. Although she loved the freedom and time she had could spend outside, Jenny missed her job.

For the first time in her married life, she started taking occasional overnight trips to her parent's. She had gone to nursing conferences before and left home. But never just to visit with family. Her parents had been divorced for several years. Jenny would visit her father and spend the weekend one month, the next month she went to visit her mother, usually when Rob was on the road and she was lonely. Even though she wasn't working now, Robe seldom let her go with him on the road. He was afraid she would get sick and he would have to bring her home and cut his trip short. Once he took her with him to the Carolinas. It wasn't Jenny that took ill, but her father. He had cancer and was in the hospital in critical condition and they had to come home immediately. After that, Rob stopped taking her with him on his business trips.

It was nice to visit her family though. Miles and years had distanced them from each other and now that was being mended. Their relationship began to grow. Not only had she renewed her relationship with her parents but aunts and uncles and cousins as well. Rob wasn't close to his family at all. His mom had passed away several years ago and his younger brother had been killed at the age of twenty-seven in an automobile accident. He had several stepbrothers and sisters, but he wasn't close to any of them. He only saw his father on special occasions and maybe every few months. Jenny wished their family could all be closer. She was an only child and had always wanted a big family with strong family ties.

By fall Jenny was really missing her job. When her cocker spaniel took ill and needed surgery to remove some tumors in her ears, Jenny asked her veterinarian if she could watch the surgery. He told her no, but that she could assist him!

"Are you sure you want to do this?" Doc asked her. "It may not be such a good idea, considering she is your pet."

"I would rather be in here with her than sitting out in the waiting room worrying about her." Jenny replied.

"Ok then, let's scrub up!"

"Don't you wear gowns? Where are your gloves?
"Jenny, this is animal surgery, you will find it quite different than what you are used to." Doc replied. "We just wash our hands good with disinfectant. There are gloves if you would like them. I prefer to be able to 'feel' what I'm doing."

Jenny didn't put gloves on either, after all, Darcie was her dog. She had been a member of the family since she was six weeks old, over ten years ago.

"There are cotton balls in the jar behind you. That's what we use for sponges." Doc pointed on the shelf behind her as he began to bluntly dissect the tumor out of Darcie's right ear. He did not take the time to control the bleeding saying he didn't need to see with his eyes, just his fingers.

"I'm not that concerned about blood loss, just how long she is under anesthesia." He said.

He saw a puzzled look on Jenny's face. She was more concerned about the blood Darcie was losing.

"There, tumor is out on this side." He said. "Would you like to close the incision Jenny?"

"YES!" She was anxious to feel the instruments in her hands again.

After only seconds of trying to close the incision, it was clear to Jenny why she was no longer in the operating room. She couldn't work fast enough, and had trouble tying the knots and hold her hands steady.

"I'm sorry Doc." She said. "Maybe you should do this after all."

"It's ok Jenny, it only needs two or three sutures, take your time. You keep working while I go check out this specimen."

As they worked on Darcie's other ear they talked a lot about Jenny's experience in the surgical unit at Community General and how it differed from his small town veterinary surgery. Doc seemed really interested and was making her feel as if he couldn't do the surgery without her. She knew that wasn't so, but appreciated his efforts all the same.

Darcie came through the surgery with flying colors and when Jenny paid the bill, Doc took half the cost off because Jenny had assisted him.

The little adventure had only made her miss her job all the more. She had been followed closely by Dr. Harris during her time off work. Every three months she would drive to university for her neurological exam. Always the first question off her lips was: "When can I return to work?" And always after her exam, Dr. Harris would give her the same answer: " Not yet Jenny." The grip strength in her hands was still very weak and her extremities still numb from the elbows down and from the knees down. Dr. Harris said it was very similar to diabetic neuropathy. The headaches were still a common occurrence and her memory was definitely not getting better.

Dr. Harris encouraged her to keep doing her exercise's to build up her strength in her legs and arms. When Jenny would ask if she were going to get worse, Dr. Harris would tell her that she had no idea of knowing for sure, but there was that possibility. It was possible that she could even end up crippled from this experience. Much, she said, would depend on Jenny's willingness to fight the muscular deterioration by doing her strengthening exercise.

Jenny and her best friend Anne had been walking nearly every day since May. Both of them lived in the country a few miles out of town in opposite directions. They met in town early each day and walked at least an hour or more. They talked about everything under the sun, from their kids, to their husbands and even the affairs of the world. They talked a lot about their faith in God and how He had blessed them and encouraged them. Anne really pushed her, both physically and spiritually. They had been like sisters for twenty-four years. They were sisters by choice and sisters in the Lord. There was nothing they didn't know about each other, nothing they didn't tell each other and nothing they couldn't say to each other. Anne noticed as they were walking one day that Jenny was dragging her right foot, stumbling over thin air every few steps. She teasingly scolded her.

"For Pete's sake girl, you are a klutz today!"

"I know, seems to be happening a lot now, I fell down walking out to the mailbox the other morning. I didn't trip over anything, just fell."

"What do I need to do? By you a pair of skates and drag you around town behind me so you don't trip over your own feet?" She teased. "You could just slide along and I'll pull you around like a puppy. You won't even have to lift up your feet."

"Oh yeah, and I suppose your name is "GRACE", like you never stumble around?" Jenny rolled her eyes at her friend.

"Jenny, that's it!" She had this look in her eyes, the one she often got when she thinks she has come up with the perfect solution for a problem. It is almost like you can see the light bulb light up over her brain. She spun around in the middle of the street and said: "WHY NOT SKATES?"

"You can't be serious!" Jenny said. "I can't stand up flat on my feet without falling down, much less roller skate!"

"I am serious! We both use to be pretty good at skating a few years ago, remember?"

"A *few* years Annie?" Jenny laughed. "Try twenty-years ago."

"Think about it Jen, we were both good at skating. You could still be getting exercise and build muscle tone. Probably even better than walking, plus you could work on coordination as well! You can't be any worse on skates

150

than you have been at walking today!" She jabbed Jenny's arm, laughing.

"I'd break my bloody neck!" Jen replied.

"As if you haven't almost done that a time or two today, you just have to slide your feet, not pick them up!" Anne was laughing so hard she could barely walk a straight line herself now. "Besides, remember, skating was fun!"

"That was twenty-years ago Anne, this is now. There isn't any place to skate anymore. We would have to drive to the nearest rink and we barely find time to meet in town for our morning walks."

"Have you been living in a cave or something? This isn't the Stone Age anymore. Tell Fred and Wilma goodbye and come on into the twenty-first century!" Anne said. "Think in-line skates. You know, roller blades! Not roller skates!"

"Ok, now I know you've lost your mind! I don't think so!"

"Come on Jen, where's that spirit of adventure you use to have?"

"Gone, the answer is NO!"

"Chicken." You are starting to get old on me! You are turning into a 'scared to live' old woman right in front of my eyes."

"NO!"

"Cluck, cluck, cluck." Anne said as she made like a chicken in the middle of the street. "We could skate one mile of our course in half the time it takes us to walk the two miles."

"Did Gary hit you over the head with the stupid stick this morning or something?" Jenny started laughing at the sight of Anne and her chicken walk. "You are being so weird, even more than usual!"

"Come on Jenny, you know you want to."

"I still think you are crazy." Jenny couldn't help but smile.

"YES!" Anne jumped for joy!

For Christmas that year, Anne bought Jenny a pair of roller blades. Jenny promptly packed them away in the closet hoping that Anne would forget them by spring.

When it turned too cold to walk outside, they went to the mall to antique malls to walk. They loved browsing the area antique shops. Nothing was more relaxing than the smell of antiques. With mellow, old music piped through the store, it was so calming. If they weren't browsing the antique shops they hit the sales in the department stores.

Good friends, you can always count on them. Anne was the best as far as Jenny was concerned. Especially when Jenny would begin to doubt that God was present in her life anymore. Anne's father had been a Baptist minister, so she was raised in the faith. She would give Jenny the spiritual pep talk she needed every time that she started to doubt God. Sometimes it helped, sometimes Jenny was still sure that God had temporarily taken His eyes off her life. Why else would it be such a mess? Anne always told her that even though she thought God had deserted her, He was still working his plan in her life. She would tell her to be patient. That seemed easy for Anne to say, hard for Jenny to do. Anne told her to count her blessings when she felt down, so Jenny began to do just that.

Jenny loved sitting outside under a starry summer night and listen to the wind chimes. That was how she preferred to count her blessings. Tonight was not a summer night, it was cold and mid-winter. But Jenny still felt the need to be outside, look at the stars and count her blessings. Facing the winter 'trapped' in the house was difficult, so Jenny started counting those blessings! She always started with her two sons. Without them, she was nothing. They had become her strength. She may be losing her marriage in the aftermath of this illness, but she would always have her sons.

To Jenny, Rob was still a blessing. When they were first married she had to depend on Rob for everything. She didn't even have her driver's license the first few years of their life together. Rob took her wherever she needed to go, the store, the laundry-mat, doctor appointments. Her existence depended upon him and he liked it that way. Once she had her license and didn't have to depend on Rob so much, he stopped being a loving husband and became a jealous and angry person. He had no reason to ever be jealous. Jenny had her hands full with two young sons and even if she had the time to, she would have never been unfaithful to Rob. She loved him with all her being and never wanted another man. But Rob was changing, starting to resent the fact that he was in his early twenties with a family when all his friends were in college and having fun. He had responsibilities, they didn't. Jenny and the boys were becoming a burden to him. That was one of the reasons she had wanted to go back to school, to take some of the stress off Rob. But he saw it differently. He saw it as her needing to be dependent and as a sign that she no longer needed him. They physical and verbal abuse began as early as the mid-seventies, not long after Jake was born. She felt the winds of change upon her marriage even then, now they had become a hurricane.

She sat in the swing out in the cold for a very long time that night, thinking and praying.

"What if I can never return to work?" She thought. That idea made her physically sick. She already missed work so much. Where else could she get the steady flow of adrenalin, the excitement and sense of accomplishment that she felt working in the operating room? Somehow, pushing a vacuum sweeper around and dusting the house just didn't give her the same feeling of self-worth as working.

"What if I can never work anywhere again?" She wondered out loud. "If I can't return to the operating room, what will I do?"

Is there a job out there that doesn't require fine motor skills, one I wouldn't even have to hold a pen for any length of time or type constantly? Where could she work that she wouldn't need her memory? Where would she go that didn't have fluorescent lighting? Her thoughts whirled around her out of control. What if she had one of her episodes of partial paralysis and didn't recover her ability to move? She couldn't expect Rob to stick around for that. Furthermore, she knew he wouldn't.

Paralysis would be hard enough for her to deal with. She knew Rob wouldn't want to be straddled with an invalid wife. She would not let that happen, no matter what she had to do.

So much for counting her blessings, somehow this blessing counting session had turned into thoughts of how to commit suicide if she had to. What was happening to her?

She needed to stop thinking this way and get busy, do something, get a life!

She dug out her incomplete sewing projects, although it was difficult to sew. She ran the needle through her finger many times not even noticing until she saw blood. She cleaned every nook and cranny of her house that winter. Closets were organized by season and color, even her sock drawer was tidy. She wasn't fast at anything. Tasks that use to take only a few hours now took a few days. But then, she had nothing but time on her hands.

Rob had been back in the Carolina's working. This time of the year was especially busy for him. Spring was on the way and everyone wanted to get new shoes on their horses so they could start to work them. He knew Jenny was getting really depressed, she cried a lot these days. He kept his calls to her short, just checking in to make sure she was ok. Once he knew she was alright, he didn't need to continue to talk to her. He had stayed away from home as long as he could and told Jenny he would be home that night.

She had a candlelight super ready when he arrived. Of course he was tired from the drive and the work, but he had missed her too. He was so confused about how he felt about her now. Mostly he just cared very much about her, even loved her still. But he was pretty sure, he was no longer in love with her and no longer wanted to remain married to her.

Jenny sensed his mood was different. After they ate she put his favorite music video in the VCR. It was by Garth Brooks, "If Tomorrow Never Comes." She was sitting on the floor in front of him, he in his favorite chair. It was an oversized rocking lounge chair. As Garth was singing the beautiful words, Rob grabbed Jenny's hand.

"Come here." He said as he pulled her onto the chair with him. Rob rarely showed strong emotions, and it had been months since he had shown Jenny any emotion at all. Tears were flowing down his cheeks as he rocked her in the chair. The words to the song, echoing in the air:

"If tomorrow never comes, will she know how much I loved her? Did I try in every way, to show her every day, that she's my only one? And if my time on earth were through and she must face this world without me, is the

156

love I gave her in the past, going to be enough to last? IF tomorrow never comes."

"Jenny, I hope you will always remember that I do love you." Rob kept repeating to her softly.

Jenny knew that night that something was going on in his heart that she couldn't understand. She later realized, that he knew then, he was going to leave her.

She began to cherish the times she spent with him, even the bad ones. Because, she knew, they were coming to an end.

The only light she found in her life was her sons. How she looked forward to the day they fell in love and married. She had such a wonderfully special relationship with them. They could sense when she was struggling and were always there for her. She loved to listen to them play their musical instruments and sing. Robbie was such an accomplished guitarist. She started going to listen to his rock band every chance she got. He had started his musical career on the drums in the high school band, switching to guitar in college. He had a natural talent for it. Jake was equally talented on the keyboard. He began on the guitar but found his true talent tickling the ivory. She was so proud of them both. She could listen to them for hours. Her sons truly taught her the meaning of unconditional love. The kind of love Christ had for us, to give his life for us. Jenny would lay down her life for her sons anytime, anywhere, for any reason. Through them she could only guess how her Heavenly Father must have felt, when he gave HIS ONLY SON to die for her sins. How great a love her Lord had, to lay down his life for her? How could she question his will in her life? How could she doubt his love? She tried not to, but she still found, she did.

Chapter Sixteen

As time passed, Dr. Harris referred Jenny to her friend, Dr. Austin. Dr. Austin was a Psychiatrist.

"I don't really think I need to see a..." Jenny was interrupted by Dr. Harris.

"I think you do." Dr. Harris began. "You have been through a lot of stuff this past two years. Professionally and personally you have been under a huge amount of stress Jenny. You have had to make so many adjustments in your life. I think you need to talk to someone about all of this. I'm asking you to do this, not forcing you."

"You really feel it is necessary, don't you?"

"If I didn't, I wouldn't have made you an appointment with her." Dr. Harris answered. "She is a good Psychiatrist Jenny; she will help you adjust to all these changes."

"Ok, I will talk to her, for you. But I can't guarantee that I will see her more than once."

"Fair enough." Dr. Harris smiled, she had better make a mental not to herself to call Dr. Austin and warn her that Jenny was strong willed and stubborn, even when you had her best interest in mind.

"When do I see this shrink?" Jenny asked her.

"Next week, and I wouldn't refer to her as a 'shrink' to her face. She is a professional, and she takes her job very seriously, like you Jenny."

"Next week? You certainly didn't want to waste any time getting me in to see her did you?" Jenny was surprised she would be seeing the shrink so soon. "You must really think I'm headed for a breakdown!"

"Jen, I don't think that at all. You have been stronger than most people might have been under the circumstances. I just don't want you to have to go this alone, not when we can help you."

"Whatever." Jenny became complacent. She would like to talk to someone though, these days it didn't feel to her as if God were listening. And she didn't feel comfortable talking to her Pastor about her personal life.

The next week she sat in the waiting area of Dr. Austin's office. As she watched everyone coming and going, she wondered what was going on in their lives. What had brought them to this point? What brought them to a 'shrink'? Were they 'flakes', or just 'overstressed' from their jobs and home life? Which one was she? She was extremely nervous, that is what she was! Never in her wildest dreams did she think she would ever end up in a 'shrink's' office!

"Hello, you must be Jenny Reed." Dr. Austin greeted her at the door.

Dr. Austin was nothing like Jenny had imagined her. Instead of being a tall, overweight woman wearing dark rimmed glasses as Jenny had imagined her. She was very small framed, although her confident manner made her seem ten feet tall. She had long brown hair and a beautiful face with an olive completion. She was a sharp dresser and seemed to project a calmness that put Jenny a little more at ease than she wanted to be.

"Yes, I'm Jenny." She grasped Dr. Austin's extended hand and noticed her fingernails were even immaculately done.

"Dr. Harris has told me a lot about you Jenny." She said. "Please, step into the office and have a seat." She opened the door to a small, dimly lit room with two chairs and a desk. What, no sofa?

Sitting down in the chair next to Jenny, not behind her desk, she placed her hand upon Jenny's and said; "Now, tell me about yourself."

"What do you want to know?" Jenny though how amusing that sounded just like a typical shrink opening line. Besides, what did she need to tell her that Dr. Harris hadn't already told her?

Reluctantly, she decided to play along.

"Tell me about your family." Dr. Austin said as she sat back in the chair.

"My husband's name is Rob, we have been married for twenty-five years. We have two sons, Robbie and Jake. Robbie is twenty-five and Jake is twenty-three. We live on a small horse farm in the country and we are very happy." She lied about the last part. SHE was happy, Rob wasn't.

"What does Rob do for a living?"

"He is a self-employed Blacksmith-Farrier-Horse trainer."

"Does he work at home?"

"Not often, he turns his shoes at home in his shop in the barn. He makes the horse shoes that he puts on his client's horses. He does specialty shoes for them. He will watch the way a horse walks and make the shoes to fit his feet." Jenny answered. "Then he goes to their farm and shoes their horses."

"Does he have to go far to do this?" She asked.

"All over the country, he travels to the Carolina's a lot. To New York State, Wisconsin, anywhere he has clients."

"Does either of your sons live at home?"

"No, they live together now in an apartment about ten miles away, after they got out of college they moved in together."

"So, when your husband is gone are you home alone?" Dr. Austin asked as she scribbled on her notepad.

"Yes."

"Does that bother you?"

"Not usually, not when he is working." Jenny's eyes began to tear up.

162

The first session with Dr. Austin focused on her family life, her parent's and hobbies, etc. It was a period of getting to know each other, For Dr. Austin, and for her. She didn't know why but she sort of liked this little woman. So, she did return for more sessions. She saw her once a week for a couple of months.

After a little while, it became clear to Jenny, the real reason she was seeing Dr. Austin.

"Jenny, how do you think you would feel if you were told you could never return to work?" She was carefully studying Jenny's eyes as she answered this question. It was something Jenny had asked herself many, many times. Yet hearing it from Dr. Austin made it sound like it was already a done deal.

"Are you trying to tell me something?" Jenny asked her as her heart began to pound and her respirations picked up. She tried to hide the fear in her eyes.

"No, but IF I were, could you face that possibility?"

"NO!" Jenny's eyes filled with tears and her hands began to tremble. It felt as if her heart were trying to jump out of her chest. She felt like she couldn't breathe, panic was overcoming her. "I HAVE to work!"

"Jenny, why do you feel you 'have' to work?"

"Because, Rob may not always be around and I need to work."

"What makes you think Rob may not always be there?"

"He just might not be and if I can't work, I won't have anything." Jenny was sobbing now. Dr. Austin handed her a box of tissue. "I am a Certified Surgical Technologist. That is what I do. That is who I am. That is what I am good at!"

"Jenny, you are also a good wife, mother, daughter and friend." She said. "You are not 'just' a C.S.T."

"But you don't understand, I'm good at my job. I'm not so good at the rest of my life."

"Think about what you just said Jenny." Dr. Austin spoke softly. "Do you feel you haven't been a good wife, or mother to your sons? Didn't you tell me that you and Rob were happy? Your sons are both well-adjusted young men. You are a success at being a mother. Why do you feel you are only good at being a surgical tech?

"Sometimes I just feel that my career is the only part of my life I am in control of."

"Maybe we need to talk more about your marriage Jenny, maybe Rob should be included in these sessions."

"I don't think so. He wouldn't come. I'm sure of that." Jenny said.

Dr. Austin could feel the wall Jenny was beginning to put up, it happened every time she tried to get her to talk about her relationship with her husband.

164

"Ok, but I suggest you consider the possibility that you may not return to work Jenny." Dr. Austin was concerned about her. "Call me if you feel the need to talk again before our next scheduled appointment."

Jenny knew Dr. Austin was holding something back from her and she didn't like it one bit. Her next appointment with Dr. Harris was in just a few days, she planned to find out what was going on. She would be the ones asking the questions at that appointment!

On the drive to University Medical Center a few days later to see Dr. Harris, all she could think about was what she was going to say. She had to know, would she or wouldn't she be able to return to work. Had Dr. Harris already told Dr. Austin that she couldn't go back to work? Is that why Dr. Austin had asked her how she felt about not working?

Jenny straightened herself in the chair as Dr. Harris entered the room. It was time. She thought about the ancient television show: "To Tell the Truth." This wasn't a game show, this was her life.

"I know we have tip-toed around the subject for the past few months, but now I'm ready, I want to hear your honest opinion." Jenny swallowed hard as her stomach churned and it became hard to talk. "Will I ever return to work as a surgical technologist or is my career over?"

There, she had asked the question, not at all sure she wanted to hear the answer.

Dr. Harris sighed deeply as if she had been expecting this moment and was relieved it had finally come. She looked at Jenny as if she were trying to see inside her mind.

"You really want an honest answer Jenny?"

"Yes, I do." Just then, Jenny knew without a doubt why she had been sent to see Dr. Austin.

"It is my professional opinion as your neurologist that you will not be able to return to your job."

Jenny's heart sank in her chest. She had known the answer before she asked the question, but it made hearing it, no less painful.

"I guess I knew that in my heart months ago, but my mind just couldn't accept it." Jenny told her. "That is why I always asked you 'when' I could return, not 'if' I could return to work."

"I knew how hard this would be for you Jenny." Dr. Harris took her hand. "That's why I wanted you to see Dr. Austin, because you always asked 'when' and not 'if'. You were in a state of denial about how serious your illness is."

"What about working in general? Is there anything I can do?"

"I don't want to discourage you Jenny. Maybe in time, you can go back to work part time." She said. "But right now, I wouldn't encourage it." Dr. Harris watched Jenny closely as she spoke to her. "You have a severe case of peripheral neuropathy. You have been left with a memory deficit." She continued to hold Jenny's hand as she watched the tears start to flow down her face. She couldn't stop now. She had to make Jenny see her situation for what it was. "Your vision is impaired by a central scotoma and you have debilitating migraine headaches. You have numbness and weakness in your arms and legs. We could go on and on with this list Jenny. I'm so sorry, I know this is hard for you, I wish I could tell you that you were going to recover, but it isn't likely.

Tears fell freely as Jenny tried to speak. "I need to ask you another question."

"Go on, what is it?"

"Will I find myself in a wheelchair from this someday?"

"I wish I could tell you that without any doubt, you will never face that possibility. But I can't Jenny." She quickly added. "I can tell you that I don't anticipate it happening. Your condition is so unpredictable. I do feel that if you work hard to keep up your muscle tone it will decrease that possibility greatly." She continued. "You are a young, vibrant woman Jenny, live your life. Take one day at a time. Yes, you will have limitations but you aren't totally crippled from this, you are disabled. There is a big difference, be grateful for what you still have."

"I know it could be sores. I read all the reports on how this chemical works and what it is capable of doing."

"Are you going to be okay with all of this?" She asked Jenny. "Or would you like me to call Dr. Austin and see if she can talk to you this afternoon?"

"No, I'm okay."

"I know you have a strong Christian faith Jenny, pray, and ask God for his help."

"I'll try." Jenny said, although praying was the last thing she felt like doing. Her world had just changed. She was no longer, nor would she ever be again, an operating room scrub nurse. Her career was over, and it had been much too short. Praying was the last thing she wanted to do.

Where was God now? She wondered. Why had he let this happen to her?

She couldn't pray, she wondered if she ever could again.

Chapter Seventeen

When Jenny returned home from her appointment with Dr. Harris that afternoon she desperately needed to talk to someone. Rob wasn't home and even if he had been, she couldn't have talked to him. They didn't talk much at all anymore, and certainly not about things that mattered. She called Anne.

"Anne, hi, it's Jenny."

"Hi! I was going to call you later to see how your appointment went, so how did it go?"

"Not good."

"Oh no, what did they say? Is there something else wrong with you?"

"No, nothing more physically." Jenny answered as she began once again to cry. She told Anne everything Dr. Harris had said.

"I'm so sorry Jen. I know how much you loved your job." She felt pain for her friend. "Is there anything I can do? Do you want me to come over and pray with you?"

"Anne, the last thing I feel like doing now is praying." Jenny said with a sarcastic tone in her voice.

"Jen, you need to draw on your faith right now, draw closer to God. HE is the only one who can help you get through this." Anne felt like she was talking to the wall. "Jen, are you listening?"

"I'm listening. Look, I have to go." Jenny just needed to be alone. Calling Anne hadn't been a good idea. She should have known she would want to pray with her. That's what Anne did.

"Ok, but don't you shut God out of your life Jenny. You know he loves you and so do I."

"I know. Goodbye." Jenny hung up the phone.

She went outside to her favorite spot in the backyard between the two tall trees in the swing and began to think.

"Draw on my faith?" She said aloud to herself. "Why does everyone tell me to draw on my faith? Can't they see I don't have faith right now? I don't know where it went. Did I leave it in a drawer or a closet somewhere? Had my faith been a victim of the term 'use it or lose it'? Maybe I can find it at the lost and found department in the local denominational church."

Now she knew she was losing it, talking aloud to herself in her backyard on a swing. Jenny was trying desperately to remember where she had left her faith, when she had lost it. She did need it now. Maybe if she remembered where she had first found it, she could remember what she did with it.

There was of course, that day with Grandpa Jake in the old church. She just knew then that she wanted to love Jesus. She and Grandpa Jake use to take walks together in the woods and in the garden. But her most vivid memory of him will always be that day in the old burned out church.

And how he had told her about Romans 8:28. She thought of that verse and what Grandpa Jake had said to her. "All things work together for the good to those that love the Lord." He told her to believe it. She was having trouble with the 'believing' these days. But the look in her Grandfather's eyes as he told her that verse is one she will never forget. She still had that old Bible, the one they had found that day. Maybe that is where she had left her faith. She rarely opened it these days. The same Bible whose pages she had worn out not so long ago. Maybe her faith was within those pages, in the Bible she left closed on the desk.

Another source of her faith in childhood had been her Aunt Florence. She was one of the first females in the pulpit in Parke County Indiana where Jenny had grown up. Aunt Florence used to preach some real fire and brimstone sermons from inside the small southern Baptist church that Jenny sometimes went to. One Easter Sunday when she was about eight-years old, she played one of the children in the church play. She gathered around at the feet of 'Jesus' played by one of the elders of the church. Now, she knew this man wasn't the real Jesus, but she felt a sense of warmth and a longing to be near the real Jesus. She didn't know how to make that commitment yet. Years passed and she had still not given her heart completely to God.

It wasn't until Jenny's son was born that she dedicated her life to the Lord. Rob's mother had taken her to church. She talked to her about the importance of dedicating little Robbie to the Lord. Jenny wanted so much to do that and when Carla asked her if she had ever truly

171

accepted Jesus as her Lord and Savior, Jenny couldn't say that she had ever really made a serious commitment to God. The Sunday service was a beautiful one and Robbie was to be christened at the end of it. As the alter call began and the choir sang "Just As I Am", Jenny was overwhelmed by the Holy Spirit. The words to the song touched her in such a way that it was as if the Lord himself had chosen it just for her. She handed baby Robbie to Carla as she made her way to the alter and committed her life to Christ. She was saved the same day baby Robbie was christened. Sitting in the swing in the wee-small hours of the morning Jenny realized she must search for her lost faith. Maybe it wasn't really lost, just left behind in the hustle and bustle of a world that moved far too fast. A blur of precious memories of her past faith was whirling around in her mind echoing for her to 'come home'. She truly needed that faith now, she need to know for certain that "All things work together for the good, to those that love the Lord."

Chapter Eighteen

Winter of 1993 came earlier than usual. And like the ever ready bunny, it seemed to last and last and last and last. Every other week Jenny would go to Community General to pick up her invalid paycheck stub and fill her prescriptions at the hospital pharmacy.

Prescriptions, prior to January 1991 the most medication she had ever taken was an occasional aspirin. She despised taking prescription drugs. As the headaches progressed even the strongest strength aspirin didn't help. Dr. Harris prescribed several different types of drugs, none of which could ease her migraines. After several months of unsuccessful attempts to control the pain they decided to try a relatively new medication that was a self-injected drug. It was only to be used when the migraine headaches had reached a point where the pain was unbearable. Within seconds of taking the injection, the migraine would disappear. However, the side effects of the injections were too much for Jenny to handle. It was as if she were injecting acid into her blood stream. She had to lie down on the sofa or bed before she started the injection. The moment she began to push the medication into her body an intense burning sensation began. She became flushed to the point it made her feel as though her body temperature were over 150%. Her head began to throb so intensely it blinded her and felt like it were ready to explode, then about thirty seconds of gut wrenching pain, the headache was gone. Every time she used it she was amazed she had survived the cure for her migraine. When she told Dr. Harris how it made her feel, she told her to stop using it. The migraines

173

returned and all Jenny could do was lie down in a dark, quiet room until they passed.

Jenny had several medications for her nerves and she hated it. She had sworn long ago that she would never use 'nerve pills'. She had no choice now; she was on edge constantly, slept little and cried a lot.

Cigarette smoke, dust and dry heat were a few of the things that made breathing difficult and irritated her eyes. She was forced to use an inhaler.

Jenny didn't accept her dependency on medications gracefully. But for the time being, she had to do what all of her doctors told her to do or face being labeled an 'uncooperative patient'. Wayne had warned them to follow the doctor's orders for their sake and for legalities. So she did, for a few months. She then grew tired of the side effects. With all the different doctors she was seeing, one would have her on a medication to increase a specific chemical in her brain while the other would have her on a medication to decrease the same chemical. Jenny decided no one knew what was good for her, except for her. So, she stopped taking all of her medications and convinced herself she was better off without them.

That decision lasted for just two days. She could barely get out of bed. The migraine she had was enough in itself to convince her. Along with it, her joints were extremely painful and stiff. All the symptoms converged upon her at once like a pack of starving wolves. Struggling to even stand up and place one foot in front of the other she imagined how ridiculous she must look on her journey to the medicine cabinet. She thought of the old cliché about how physicians and nurses made the worst patients, always trying to heal themselves. It was true, self-diagnosis and self-treatments were common place among healthcare professionals. Even though this plan didn't work, Jenny was still determined that someday she would find something else that would work for her. After all the legal process was over she would seek out a qualified Horologist and Homeopath to help her. She would be prescription drug free someday.

Although at this time, workman's compensation was paying for her doctor bills and prescription drugs, Jenny still worried about the continued added expenses. How would she and Rob manage without her income? She had been working long shifts and talking extra call just to make ends meet. Now, they were on a restricted income from her point of view.

What if they lost the case against CLS and had to pay all of these bills themselves? They could lose the farm! Plus, she depended on her insurance from Community General. Rob was self-employed and had no insurance. No wonder she couldn't sleep at night! No wonder when she did she had nightmares! She would dream of being in a wheelchair and too weak to stand. She called and called but no one came to help her. The horses were hungry and needing fed. Jenny couldn't get to the barn. She couldn't get out of the door to the house with the wheelchair. Then she would be in a dark room with no one around. It was like she was in a spotlight yet in total darkness, in the wheelchair. The dream came much too often and she began to fear sleep. Mr. Stevens better win this case for them. He had already found proof that CLS knew they had a problem with the sterilization of the gowns.   There was proof that they had exceeded government regulations and standards. They knew they were guilty, we all knew they were guilty. However, they were still arguing that the chemicals did not cause our illness. All twelve of us girls just 'happened' to get sick at the same time. Mr. Stevens had to find the most influential and knowledgeable experts to examine his clients. He had already had the most prominent Neurologist see them in New York, but he needed more. More expert testimony on their behalf that the chemical exposure to Ethylene Oxide and Ethylene Chlorohydrin had indeed caused their problems.

Chapter Nineteen

"Is this Mrs. Jenny Reed?" The voice at the other end of the telephone line asked.

"Yes, this is Jenny." She answered. "Who is this?"

"Hello Mrs. Reed, this is Molly Winter. Mr. Stevens' legal assistant. I'm calling to see if you would be free this morning. Mr. Stevens would like to meet with you."

"I did have plans as a matter of fact, but I suppose I could change them given a little time."

"I realize this may be a bit of inconvenience, but it is very important." Molly said.

"Has CLS made an offer?" Always Jenny's first thought.

"No, they haven't." She replied. "Do you remember Mr. Stevens talking to you about Dr. Brady? He is the Toxicologist from California. The one Mr. Stevens was hoping to enlist as an expert witness in your case."

"Yes, vaguely."

"He is here and Mr. Stevens would like you to meet with the two of them in the lobby at Community General at 11:00 am."

"Why at Community General?"

"I understand that prior approval has been arranged for you to take Mr. Stevens and Dr. Brady on a tour of the surgical unit." Molly said. "They want you to simulate a mock surgical case for them."

"STOP! Just give me a minute to think!" Jenny had not heard a thing after Molly had said the words 'tour of the surgical unit'. Jenny hadn't been back in the operating room since she walked out of it on May 7th 1993. That was over eight months ago!

"I can't do this. I can't take them on a tour of the unit. You will have to get someone else."

"Jenny, this is extremely important to your case. Why can't you do it? Is something wrong?"

"YES, something is wrong, this is all wrong! I can't do it! I can't go back into the operating room. I'm sorry. Tell Wayne he will have to get one of the other girls to do this."

Jenny hadn't been back to the operating room sense the day she walked out and was put on workman's compensation. She was now on total disability and would never be able to return to the career she loved. Four of the other 'rash rats' were also on disability. Lisa, Linda, Melissa and Jamie along with Jenny had been diagnosed with peripheral neuropathy, migraines, lupus and multiple sclerosis.

Jenny couldn't face walking back through the operating room doors.

"There isn't time to find someone else Jenny." Molly said. "Dr. Brady has traveled a long way for you girls and we need your help."

She was trapped, just like a true 'rat'. Well, why not? She was a 'rash rat' after all. She just needed to dig deep and find the strength to walk those halls with her head up and her shoulders back.

"I'll be there." She told Molly.

The drive to Community General seemed to take forever, she wasn't sure she could do what was being asked of her. She really, really, didn't want to. What she wanted to do was turnaround and go back home. It was hard enough to make her weekly pilgrimage to pick up her monthly prescriptions at the hospital pharmacy. The 'odor' of the corridors in the hospital alone was enough to fill her with longing and desire to take her place along some gifted surgeon, helping to heal a human life. Anytime she went into a hospital, any hospital she would begin conversations with anyone dressed in surgical uniforms. She would ask if they worked in the operating room, did they like it? How long had they been there? What new procedures were they doing? It reassured her to talk about it.

In the parking garage, Jenny prayed, asking God to give her strength to do what she had to do today, if not for her, for Lisa and the rest of the 'rash rats'.

Wayne and Dr. Brady were waiting on her as they sipped coffee in the main lobby.

"Jenny, glad you could make it." Wayne stood to greet her when she walked in. "This is Dr. Charles Brady; he is a toxicologist from San Diego, California. I told you about him earlier."

"Pleased to meet you." Jenny extended her hand to him.

"Please, call me Chuck, and the pleasure is mine Jenny. I only wish it had been under better circumstances." He replied.

Turning to Wayne he asked. "Is there a place we can go so I may be able to talk to Jenny and examine her? We only need a bit of privacy, an exam room isn't necessary."

"Guess we better ask Jenny that, she is the tour guide." Wayne replied as he gave Jenny a questioning glance.

"Simply questions?" Jenny asked.

"Simply questions Jenny, it won't take long." Dr. Brady smiled.

"There is a chapel down the corridor. There is usually no one in there this this time of day."

"That's fine with me as long as you are comfortable with it."

If only he knew how many hours Jenny had knelt at the altar in this very chapel on her lunch breaks. It was a beautiful chapel, soft lighting and even-toned colors that made you feel at ease. . Today, she didn't feel at all comfortable. It wasn't Dr. Brady making her feel that way. It was being in the chapel, any chapel.

Jenny directed him to a bench next to the altar. Wayne sat across from them. Dr. Brady sat next to Jenny on the bench. He began to ask her questions.

"I want you to tell me in your own words Jenny, how did this happen?" He asked.

"The residue of the chemicals, Ethylene Oxide and Ethylene Chlorohydrin were in the cuffs of the gowns that came pre-package in our custom hip packs and custom arthroscopy packs. What it boils down to is that when the gowns were shipped form CLS the cuffs of the gowns still contained a high residue of chemicals. They were much higher than the government and OSHA safety standards allow. I wore the gowns, my arms broke out, my health deteriorated and I'm on total disability. That covers it."

"Tell me about the rash, what did it look like? Did you feel anything unusual? Was there anything that was specific about the rash that you can remember? He continued with the questions.

"I didn't know at the time what I was experiencing. At first I thought it was just a case of nerves. So much had been going on in my life. My arms burned as if there were small coals of hot charcoal inside my bones. They felt like they were on fire from the inside out. They itched all of the time and when I wore anything long sleeved it irritated them." Jenny answered. "Oh, and the had small water

181

blisters all over them. The worse part of the rash was directly over the area where *I* wore my cuffs."

"What do you mean where you wore your cuffs?" He questioned her. "When you said that it sounded as if there were something specific about how you wore your cuffs from the all the rest."

"There is. The other girls always pulled their cuffs 'down' when they put their gloves on." Jenny tried to show him on her own hands where the other girls wore their gown cuffs. "They wore their cuffs down midways of their hands. That is where their rash was worse, from the middle of their hands to where the cuff ended. Not mine. I always pulled my cuffs 'up' instead." Once again Jenny motioned to her arms to show him how her gown cuffs were worn. "On my arms, the rash was directly at my wrist and the exact length of the cuffs. My rash was the only one that didn't begin mid-hand. That is how they came to the conclusion that it was the cuffs of the gowns holding the residual from the chemicals." Jenny explained. "The water blisters were in the direct area of the banded cuffs on all of us in proportion to where each of us wore her cuffs."

"What did the blisters look like? Describe them for me."

"They were small and close together, not big. When they faded they left a red and blotchy rash where they had been."

"Jenny, when you opened the custom packs did you notice anything unusual or out of the ordinary?"

"Yes, there was always this odor. It was very distinct. It made my eyes and the inside of my nose sting. They burned, and it made me sneeze. It kind of reminded me of when I was a little kid. Did you ever put a copper penny in your mouth? I did once. It was that same kind of prominent chemical twang."

Dr. Brady grasped both of her hands in his, looking at Wayne he began to shake his head and laugh. Jenny was confused, he was laughing?

"She couldn't have answered that question more perfectly." Still laughing, he hugged Jenny. "I'm sorry. I know this isn't a laughing matter at all. It's just that I could have tricked you into answering that question the way I wanted you to. I could have directed the questions to you in such a way as to influence your answers. I didn't. Yet, you described it on your own perfectly. Jenny, you have definitely had an overdose of Ethylene Oxide and Ethylene Chlorohydrin. Tell me, how do you feel now? What are your most common symptoms?" He asked.

"Mostly muscle weakness, neuropathy, headaches, visual weakness and very forgetful."

"What medicines are you on?"

Jenny went over her long list of medications with him.

"I would like to see the surgical unit now. I'll have more questions when we are inside the unit." He told her.

"About that, is there any way you can do this part without me?" She asked. "Nothing personal but this is going to be hard for me. I haven't been back inside the operating room in eight months. I really miss being part of the surgical team and I'm not ready emotionally to face this."

"I do understand your position Jenny." He said. "But we need you to guide us through this and help us shed some light on the inside conditions surround the surgeries where these custom packs were used."

Jenny looked at Wayne with pleading eyes, but his response was the same as Dr. Brady's had been.

"You have to do this Jenny. We need you. I want you to show us where the packs are stored. They we need to make a video and do a mock set up of a case." Wayne said. "We have clearance from the hospital administration to do whatever we need. They have given us use of room #8. Jenny, this is going to be a great help in your case. I promise you. If this goes to court, what we do here today will be vital to the case."

"Let's do it and get it over." Jenny said.

Once on the second floor they approached the sliding glass window that opened into the front office of the surgical unit. Jane, the unit secretary was busy at her computer when she noticed Jenny.

"Hello stranger! What are you doing? Are you lost or did you finally decided to come back to work?" Jane asked.

"I'm lost. Is Barbara here? I need to talk to her." Jenny would have loved to say she was here to return to work.

"Yes, in her office. I'll get her for you." Jane said as she pressed the intercom button. "Barbara, could you come to the front window? You won't believe who is here to see you."

"I'll be right there." Barbara answered.

Moments later she arrived in the front office. "Hello Jenny." She said in a dry, professional manner. "I've been expecting you."

Jane was trying to listen to the conversation. She had not been made aware that Barbara was expecting Jenny today.

S"I understand you are giving a little tour of our facility this afternoon." Barbara said as she looked Dr. Brady over. He was strikingly handsome, tall with jet-black hair and eyes so blue they appeared to be sapphire stones. Barbara was a divorced, middle aged woman.

"Yes, I am." Jenny said. "This is Dr. Brady from California. Of course, you already know MR. Stevens." Jenny was aware of the tension in the air between herself and Barbara. It seemed both Dr. Brady and Wayne had also picked up on it. There was no love lost between them. When Jenny could no longer scrub it was Barbara that suggested she be put to work down in central supply, where the Ethylene Oxide sterilizer was. But then Barbara wasn't

185

the most adored person to anyone she knew. The term 'fair' was not in her vocabulary.

"Dr. Brady, pleased to meet you." Barbara extended a hand to him. "Mr. Stevens, always a pleasure."

"Jenny, show these gentleman where they need to go to change from their suites into our hospital scrubs. Then meet me inside by the lounge." Barbara tried to flex her authority by giving Jenny orders as if she still worked for her.

Jenny showed them the way to the doctor's locker room, giving them keys to the visitor's locker. She then showed them where they would find suitable scrub suites in their size. She instructed them to cover their shoes with the shoe covers and put a hat over their heads before they left the locker area.

"I'll meet you inside in a few minutes." Jenny told them, leaving them to change her own clothes.

Jenny walked inside the familiar nurse's locker room and over to her own locker. Hers was next to Lisa's. They still retained their lockers, until the case was over, even though they were both now on disability. She stood silently for a few minutes, reminiscing. She remembered all the good times they had in that locker room. They often pulled practical jokes on each other. Once Jenny had cleaned out her locker and shoved everything inside Lisa's locker. When Lisa opened her locker the next morning, trash, shoes and books came falling out on top of her. She laughed as Jenny told her that she didn't think she would even notice because her locker was always a mess. Now, eight months later, standing in front of her locker, she was talking to herself. Unaware anyone was even around.

"What is my locker combination?" Jenny asked herself out loud. She didn't expect an answer.

"Maybe if you showed up for work more than once a year you would know the combination!" Sharon said from behind her.

"Oh my gosh! Sharon!" Jenny shouted and threw her arms around her dear friend. "How are you?"

"I'm fine, question is, how are you?"

"Surviving I guess, one day at a time. I really miss you guys though, even Dr. Lawrence!" Jenny laughed.

"Boy have you been gone too long! When are you coming back Jenny? We miss you!"

"I don't know, soon I hope." Jenny fibbed. She wasn't ready to tell anyone that she had been put on total disability. No one knew that for certain but Jenny, her doctors and her lawyer.

"So what are you doing here today? Visiting?" Sharon asked.

"No, I'm taking Dr. Brady from California and Mr. Stevens on a tour of the unit."

"Really? That's interesting. Is there a reason for this tour?" Sharon innocently asked. Sharon was one of the good guys, the ones in her corner.

"There is, but I'm not free to tell you about it." Jenny answered.

"I understand. Hey, call me, we can do lunch sometime."

"Okay."

"Bye Jenny, don't let this get to you." Sharon walked back through the locker room door waving at Jenny as she left.

"Don't let it get to me? Wait... Sharon!" Jenny tried to catch her friend, but she was still in street clothes and couldn't enter the operating room yet.

That had sounded like a warning to Jenny.

After finally getting her locker to respond to her touch, Jenny changed into scrubs. Oh how she had missed wearing scrubs. Not that it was a fashion statement, far from it. She just loved the uniform and what it represented. As she placed her hand on the door she felt like the little engine that could... I can do this, I can do this...I can do this. She entered.

How very fortunate for her that the first person she saw was Dr. Roberts. Rob, as everyone called him, was her favorite anesthesiologist. When she had been told she needed a spinal tap to confirm the diagnosis of MS, she had called Rob. She didn't want to have it done at University Medical Center. She knew it would be an intern or resident poking a needle into her back. And while they needed to learn, the last thing Jenny needed right now was someone prodding around on her practicing their technique. She agreed to have the spinal tap done only if Rob could do it at Community General and send the fluid to the University Multiple Sclerosis Lab. She had assisted Rob many times on spinal taps and never saw him miss once. Rob agreed, and was successful on the first try as usual. She was grateful for his help.

"Hi Rob!" Jenny caught his attention. "I hear congratulations are in order! You are a new Daddy again!" He was shocked to see her.

"Jen! Are you back?" He gave her a big hug. "God it's good to see you! You look good! How do you feel? Are you getting better?" He was full of questions.

"Actually, I'm not back. I'm just here for a short visit."

"Well, yeah, I have two daughters now! Isn't that great?" He was so proud of his children.

"Yes, it is great. I told you about taking Missy on vacation. Every time you do, she comes back pregnant!" She teased him.

"So true, those vacations, you know how they are!" He said. "It's sure been good to see you, we miss you around here." Glancing at this wrist watch he continued.

"Darn, I really have to run. My patient is ready to go to the room. Take care of yourself!" He hugged her goodbye.

"Thanks, I will."

Just then Wayne and Dr. Brady came into the hallway. They looked rather funny in their scrubs, especially Wayne.

"Don't you two look cute?" She said jokingly. Just being back inside the operating room seemed to bring back the old Jenny, sharp witted, happy and in control.

"Do I look like a doctor?" The attorney in Wayne just couldn't resist the crack.

"Let's pretend you do, so you will blend in." Jenny said. "You know how well doctors and lawyers generally mix. Like oil and water and you are outnumbered in here."

Turning to Dr. Brady she asked. "Where would you like to go first?"

"Show me the area where you normally scrub your arms to prepare for a case."

Jenny was about to continue on with her tour when Barbara tried to take charge of the situation.

"I see you gentlemen found your way inside." Barbara said to them. "I will be with you in just a few minutes to escort you. First I need to take care of a few things."

"That won't be necessary. We have Jenny to guide us. IF we need you we will call for you." Dr. Brady spoke up. Jenny was sure she liked this man now.

"Whatever." Barbara said as she left in a snit. "Jenny, you will find everything you need in room #8."

"Ok, let's get this over with." Jenny began walking along side of the two men in the hall. She pointed out the scrub sinks to Dr. Brady that were in between the two joining operating rooms. There were twelve operating rooms in the department. Always in two's and always with a scrub sink between them. They were drawing stares from everyone they passed.

"Our surgical unit is sat up in a basic square design. As I showed you there is a scrub area between each two rooms." As they approached the area between rooms #5 and #6, Melissa was just beginning to scrub. Jenny stopped to introduce her to Dr. Brady.

"Melissa, this is Dr. Brady, he is the toxicologist that Wayne told us about."

Dr. Brady began to question Melissa as she scrubbed her arms. She and Wayne stepped across the hall to give them some privacy.

"Are those the 'space suites' that are worn during the total joint replacement surgeries you told me about?" Wayne asked as he pointed to the garments Melissa was wearing.

"Yes, they are."

"Would you mind suiting up in one of those for me to take a video of?" He asked. "I would like to see the complete outfit, down to the helmets and the oxygen hookup in the video."

"Sure, if I can remember how to put one on, it has been awhile." She said. "And you will have to help me with the oxygen tank."

"Sure."

Once Jenny was completely gowned up in the total replacement suite, Wayne told her. "Turn around slowly so I can capture every aspect of this suit on video."

Jenny did as instructed. Wow, it had been a long time. Now however, she was feeling a bit claustrophobic. She had never felt that before wearing one of the suites. Now she couldn't wait to get out of it.

"Good enough." Wayne said. "Let's get you out of that and move on to the surgical room."

"I'm more than ready! Unhook me so I can get this fish tank off!"

Wayne helped her out of the suite as Dr. Brady caught back up with them. He had finished talking to Melissa.

Inside room #8 it seemed that every case Jenny had ever done in that particular room was flashing back to her. One after another they kept popping up in her mind like a series of flash bulbs blinking in the dark. It was so amazing, so many good memories, so many fun cases and a few bad ones as well.

She remembered one particularly funny incident. She had been working an extra-long shift that day. Every case she had done that day had been with the same surgeon. He was very intelligent, book-smart. However, how he had become a surgeon was a mystery to Jenny and everyone else who had worked with him. When it came down to identifying certain trouble spots, he would ask his scrub nurse what to do! Even when it came to identifying the difference between an artery and a vein! It had been a long, hard day. Jenny had been standing at that operating table with him for more than five hours straight. It was getting late and the surgeon had asked her for an instrument. When she handed it to him, he would then ask for something completely different. He was getting on Jenny's last nerve. She was slapping the instruments into his hands so hard that they were making such a loud popping sound her circulating nurse could hear them on the other side of the room. Jenny could handle his indecision about which instrument to use. She even overlooked his clumsiness as he constantly dropped things on the floor. But when he 'whistled' at her for an instrument, like she was a dog, well that did it! Last nerve, snapped. Jenny slapped the instrument into his hand so hard that he dropped it and began shaking his hand in pain!

"Dammit Jenny! What is wrong with you?" He growled.

"What is wrong with 'ME'?" Jenny was seething. "I'll tell you what is wrong with 'ME'! If you need something just ask me! But don't you ever, I mean EVER, whistle at me like I am a dog again!" Jenny's face was flushed with anger, or exhaustion. Just then, Kelly walked into the room, unsuspecting of what was going on. She soon sensed the tension.

"Hi Jen, do you need a break?" She asked.

"I'll say she does!!" The surgeon quickly replied before Jenny could even say yes.

"I sure do!"

"Truce?" The doctor asked her?

"Truce." Jenny answered.

Jenny's daydreaming was interrupted by Dr. Brady.

"Jenny, where would you normally be during the preparation of one of these cases?"

"Here, at this table, preparing my instruments." Jenny answered as she walked to the long sleek silver table in the corner of the room. "It's called a back-table, because it is directly behind the scrub nurse at her back during the surgery."

"Could you pretend you are opening up sterile supplies and show me how close you would be standing?"

"I can do better than that." Jenny said as she went to the warmer in between the rooms and pulled out a pack of sterile gowns.

"Wait!" Dr. Brady said. "We don't want you opening anything with chemicals in it."

"It's okay. These were steam sterilized, not by chemicals." She said as she began to open them. Wayne was taping the whole thing with his video camera.

Dr. Brady continued with the questions. How long did most procedures take? How long was the scrub nurse in the room before the surgeon actually came in? How long after the surgery was over was she still wearing her scrub gown?

"I think that is probably enough." Wayne finally said. "Let's get dressed and get out of here. We will meet in the corridor."

As Jenny walked back through the halls of the surgical unit on her way to the locker room, she tried to embrace every emotion she was feeling. She took every sight and smell into her memory. She looked at the door number and into the window of each room as she passed them. She slowly walked away from this part of her life. She knew, she would never walk the halls of a surgical unit again as a surgical technologist. She began to walk fast, faster, as her emotions were beginning to overwhelm her. The tears began to fall. Everyone she passed spoke to her, asking questions. She couldn't talk. She had to get out of there!

Inside the locker room she cleared out the rest of the items she had left there. She had no plans to return. On the front of her locker two magnets held up a typed memo that both she and Lisa had posted to their lockers. "Don't let the buzzards get you down." It had been their class motto. She took it off and threw it in the trash. The buzzards not only had her down, they were circling.

Chapter Twenty

"Are you going to the chapter meeting this month?" Lisa asked Jenny.

"I don't know, what do you think about it?" Jenny answered as she twisted the phone cord around her fingers. She really didn't want to, but if Lisa did, she would go with her.

"It just makes me miss being a part of that whole scenario." Lisa replied.

"I know, listening to the idle gossip, new procedures and equipment that I wouldn't know if I saw it. Just makes me sad."

"Me too." Lisa said.

"So, are you going?"

"Maybe."

"Did you ever get your notice from national about our membership dues?" Jenny asked.

"Yeah, I'm not sure what I'm going to do about that either."

"What do you mean?"

"I'm just not sure I want to renew my membership. I can't work as a surgical tech, so why pay dues to belong to national? Why keep up the cost of membership. Especially when you have to keep up your continuing education credits." Lisa said. "It's crazy. What's the point? We can't work."

"So, have you made up your mind about the meeting then?"

"Yes, let's skip it."

After their conversation Jenny thought again about dropping her membership to national. She couldn't believe she was even considering it! Was this the same Jenny Reed that served for six consecutive years on national committee for the Association of Surgical Technologists? Traveling to Denver twice a year to meetings? Was this the same Jenny Reed that worked hard at recruiting new members in an effort to give them a stronger voice in congress? Wasn't it she who had always tried to raise the standards of her profession? She had written several articles in their national magazine for publication. She attended local and state meetings monthly and was a delegate in the congressional meetings that were held once a year. Was she seriously thinking of dropping her membership?

Part of her wanted so much to continue on with the membership and go to the meetings. She wanted to keep working for a higher standard of professionalism and education. But yet, she knew she had to let go of the past. She was no longer a surgical technologist.

Damn CLS for what they had taken from her.

Chapter Twenty One

Just when Jenny was beginning to feel somewhat secure that her condition wasn't going to get worse, something else happened. She started having what she thought were seizures. After a check-up with Dr. Harris, she found out they were not seizures. Dr. Harris wasn't quite sure what they were and felt they may be panic attacks. Jenny called them her 'earthquake blues'. Each time she had one she would lose a little more ground physically. Sometimes they were brought on by her painful muscle spasms. Her muscles would jerk and contract so badly that the pain was excruciating. It would then cause Jenny to start hyperventilating and her pulse would increase. Sometimes she would even pass out. Other times, being upset could cause them. She and Rob fighting often caused a case of her 'blues'.

Whatever caused them, each time she became weaker. Dr. Harris suggested that she have a nerve biopsy done. A small section of her sural nerve from her left ankle was surgically removed under local anesthesia. A few weeks later the results came in. It confirmed deterioration to the mylenated sheath that surrounds her nerve fibers. One of her many MRI's had also shown to be abnormal, showing atrophy in her brain.

It didn't help to cry. Jenny had given up on that, months ago. Matter of fact, she seldom cried at all any more or showed any emotion. She stopped praying, she seldom saw her friends and family, she just stayed to herself. If she couldn't tolerate herself, how could she expect anyone else to tolerate her?

She was angry, very angry. But who was she angry with? Who was there to yell and scream at? Who was there to blame? Anger and hatred weren't emotions that she had experience with. Nor did she want to. One night while lying in bed she turned to Rob and said: "Rob, are you asleep?"

"No, why?"

"I want you to promise me something. I know that neither of us likes to talk about what has been going on with the lawsuit. It is too frustrating. But I want you to promise me that if for any reason, something happens to me before this whole thing is through, that you and the boys will see it to the end."

"Jenny, nothing is going to happen to you." Rob snapped. "Stop talking that way."

"I hope not, but just in case, promise me." She said. "Please don't let CLS get away with what they have done to me. It isn't that I want their money. I would rather have my health back, but I don't want them to go unpunished for what they have done to me, to the rest of the girls."

"I promise." Rob said.

"Rob, have you noticed that white van that constantly drives down the road?"

"Yeah, but I can't figure out where they live or what they are doing out here. They always stop about a half mile down the road and just sit there." He said.

"I know, I told Wayne about it and he thinks it is CLS representatives. He thinks they are watching us, taking photos of our activities and listening in on our phone calls."

'That's ridiculous Jen."

"No Rob, it isn't. We are suing a multi-billion dollar company for no less than twelve million dollars. Are you so narrow minded that you can't see what this is worth to them?" Jenny was getting angry. "Not to mention if word of this got out, it could ruin their reputation and affect their company far worse than a twelve million dollar lawsuit."

"So think they are following us?" Rob was starting to believe Jenny had gone off her rocker from the pressure.

"Yes, that is exactly what I'm saying." Jen said. "So please, follow this thing through for me if I can't."

"Whatever." Rob said sarcastically. "Get some sleep."

Jenny was right. A few months later Wayne presented photos of each of his clients to them that CLS had sent to him. He had a photo of Jenny, taking care of the horses when she wasn't supposed to be well enough to. One of Melissa, roller skating with her daughter. Some of Lisa, bowling with Jim. Each of them doing normal daily activities yet, CLS was trying to say that because of this, none of them were seriously ill. Wayne stressed to them again to be very careful of what they did until after the lawsuit was settled.

Rob apologized to Jenny for not believing her and assured her that he would follow this through to the end no matter what. She felt better as she knew this could drag out indefinitely. They had the money and time on their side. We were now playing a waiting game with them. It had already been two years. Their future was totally in the hands of CLS. Now, the CLS company got to have their doctors examine the 'rash-rats'.

Medical papers had already been prepared with the statistical information concerning the twelve nurses. Their statistics had already been published in several medical journals including the Neurology Journal of Medicine. Who would survive and live out their lives as they were put on this earth to do? How many would get leukemia? How many would get cancer? How many would end up in a wheel chair from MS? The rest of Jenny's life would be spent waiting for the other shoe to drop. She would never be at peace.

Chapter Twenty Two

Days turned into weeks and weeks to months, then months to years. They all grew tired of attorney's, legal tactics and especially doctors. They had truly been considered guinea pigs for the medical field.

It seemed as though everyone else but Jenny was in control of her life. She felt completely out of control. Being in the midst of a large legal battle such as this was much like being in the eye of a hurricane. The world spun around you at top speed spewing out debris and pieces of your life. All you could do was stand back and watch helplessly as the destruction whirled around you in every direction. It left no part of her life untouched. She was trapped in a place where time was standing still, in the eye of the hurricane.

So many things had happened. Jenny was still on total disability, so their finances were squeaky tight. Yet they were to a point where they had to do something about their one hundred-twenty year old farm house that the foundation was caving out from under. Rob needed a new barn. But nothing could be done when you are unemployed and disabled.

Not only were the normal things in her life falling apart, so was her marriage. Rob was gone more than he was home now. He spent less than a week a month with her. She had gained weight due to the steroids she had been put on and she was irritable and hard to get along with.

Rob couldn't see that most of Jenny's moodiness was due to the huge amount of medications she was taking. While she had stabilized, she still hadn't accepted her limitations or learned to live with them. She was full of self-pity and anger. It wore on his nerves and he had begun seeing another woman. He kept it from Jenny, he would tell her after the lawsuit was final.

In August of 1994, Jenny's father passed away. The day he died, she had sat in the intensive care unit with him at University Medical Center. He could hear her, but he couldn't respond. She began to sing "Amazing Grace." It was her father's favorite hymn. After the first verse, he opened his eyes and looked right at her. She was holding his hand.

Jenny was shocked when he opened his eyes because he hadn't opened them in over twenty-four hours. "Daddy, I'm here. You know how much I love you, don't you?" She asked, not sure he could hear her.

He nodded his head, ever so slightly as the tears rolled down his cheek. He could hear her! He tried to speak and couldn't.

"Are you trying to say you love me too?" She asked.

He tipped his head again, as the tears fell.

Once again he tried to speak. Jenny almost thought she heard him say the word, 'song'.

"You want me to keep singing your song?" She asked.

He nodded one more time, and closed his eyes.

Jenny began to sing her father's song to him as he drifted off into sleep. A few moments later Rob and the boys came into the room. Jenny's aunt Betty, her father's sister and her husband were there. Jenny's stepmother came in too. They all watched together as the line went flat on the cardiac monitor. Her father breathed his last breath.

His funeral was a military one. He had served in the Army in Korea. The twenty-one gun salute echoed through Jenny's very soul. God, where are you? Why did you take my dad? Even as she had sat by his deathbed singing the song he loved so, she felt almost untouched. She had distanced herself so far from God.

Her father's death really took a toll on her, but she didn't have a chance to mourn long. Only two months later, her mother was diagnosed with laryngeal cancer. Was she being punished? What had she done to make God so angry with her? She grew angry with Him!

Her mother's surgery was in mid-October. She was in the intensive care unit for twenty-eight days before she was taken off the respirator. Jenny had to bring her mother home to help her recover. She moved her to a town only a few miles away so she could be near to her and take her to her doctor appointments.

She and Rob barely talked at all.

Spring of 1995 brought hope that at least her dealings with CLS would be over. It was long past time that her dealings with CLS be a thing of the past. It had been a dark shadow on her life for far too long. So much tragedy had befallen her in such a short period of time. Only five-years had passed and her life had changed so drastically. They settled out of court for far less than they should have with CLS. It can only be said that they 'resolved' their issue. After Wayne's law firm took the biggest share of the settlement, she barely had enough to pay her medical bills and put some money back. But it was over, and for that she was grateful. She could now move on with her life, though she would never be able to forget.

Lisa had intestinal cancer as a result of the exposure. She had two surgeries in two years before the lawsuit had ended. Lisa was dear to Jenny. She prayed she wouldn't lose her too.

Melissa, Linda and Jenny were all diagnosed with MS and Lupus.

In the fall of 1996 after twenty-seven years of marriage, Rob left Jenny for another woman. He had met her during his travels. She was a woman who was healthy.

To say she was devastated when he left would have been an understatement. She didn't leave the house for weeks at a time. She was angry with the world, angry at God. She had one panic attack after the other, often ending up in the emergency room of the nearest hospital for treatment. She had lost forty-pounds and had no will to live.

Jenny tried to take her own life a few months after Rob had left. The frightening part was that she didn't remember even doing it. She had fallen so out of touch with God, now she was losing touch with reality. After her attempted suicide, she knew she had to get control of her life. Not for her sake, but for the sake of her sons. What she did to them when she had attempted suicide was unforgivable. No son should lose his mother to suicide. For their sake, she had to get a grasp on reality.

The first thing she did was toss out all her medications but for a few. She was literally afraid to have any medicine in the house. She went to a Herbologist and began to take herbs to heal her body. The herbs didn't have the side effects of the prescription drugs. Her head began to clear and so did her thinking. She no longer lived in a fog each day. Instead of blaming God for her life falling apart, she gave her life back to him.

Jenny hadn't been in the barn in over a year, sense Rob left. It was time. She bravely walked to the barn one fall morning, knees shaking. She was going to face Rob's ghost head on.

With tears streaming down her face she began to clear out Rob's workroom in the barn. She threw away anything and everything Rob had left behind. She only saved the ointments and dressings for the horses because someday, Jenny intended to have her own horse. She was talking to God as she cleaned, asking him to fill her with his strength. She needed strength to move on with her life and carve out a life without Rob in it. Jenny planned to make Rob's work room, her new tact room. She was doing just fine until she came across one of Rob's gloves. Emotions overwhelmed her to the point of driving her to rage, she fell apart.

"I hate you! Do you hear me God? I hate you! And I hate Rob!"

Jenny couldn't believe the words that had just came out of her mouth. She had been trying so hard to mend her broken faith and restore her relationship with God.

She fell to her knees in the barn and sobbed. She had never before in her life cried as hard as she did that moment. She screamed and wailed in pain, emotional pain so overwhelming that she couldn't catch her breath. Finally, she fell prostrate on her face on the ground.

"Jesus, I am so sorry! I don't hate you, I need you! I need your comfort, I need your grace. I need your love! I need mercy! Please, have mercy on me and forgive me for saying that I hate you. Forgive me for being so angry with you."

A peace fell upon Jenny as she felt the Holy Spirit within her heart, whispering to her.

"I forgive you my child, now you must forgive yourself, and Rob."

Jenny lay on the dirt floor of the barn for almost an hour. She continued to cry as she sought her savior with her whole heart. When she stood, she felt like a completely different Jenny. She was now assured that God was with her and she would be just fine. Not only would she survive, she would conquer. She would conquer her fears, the depression and her loneliness. She would overcome it all, with God's help.

He was the master potter and she was the clay. She asked him to mold her, make her all that he wanted her to be. All the pain and suffering she had endured had a reason behind it. Something good would come out of the chaos she called her life.

As she grew nearer to God, he drew nearer to her. He showed her that all the things she had been through had a reason. He got her attention. Jenny had been relying on other people for all her needs and not God. She had worshipped Rob to the point of making him a god in her life, putting him before her true God, Jesus.

Jenny learned that all she really needed in her life was to put God first. Once she 'came home' to her Savior and found her faith, Jenny was a changed person. She learned to appreciate each day of her life. She learned to be thankful for the things she 'could' still do instead of dwelling on the things she no longer could do. She learned to have joy in her life.

God blessed Jenny for her faithfulness. Both Robbie and Jake were born again Christians, 'after' Jenny and Rob had divorced. Out of her tragedy, came great joy.

Just as Grandpa Jake had said it would: "All things work together for the good, to those that love the Lord and are called to his purpose."

About the Author:

Ruthann Keller lives in Jay County, Indiana with her husband, Jack and their three dogs and two cats.

She is a retired surgical technologist and is now focusing only on serving God through publishing a church newsletter each month and writing.

A woman of faith, Ruthann hopes to reach those who struggle with their faith as they walk through the trials and tribulations of this life we live.

Made in the USA
Columbia, SC
17 December 2017